Praise for THE ACCIDENT[AL...]

"Frank Lentricchia's new novel ranks [...] of a high
order – funny, fast-moving and hot-blooded. It's also the kind of
novel that will appeal to readers who like their fiction to carry
depth and range."
—DON DeLILLO

"*The Accidental Pallbearer* is a brilliant piece of fiction, and a page
turner to boot, able to stand shoulder to shoulder with the best
writing in America today."
—JAY PARINI

"*The Accidental Pallbearer* deserves to be read alongside the best liter-
ary detective fiction of our time. Lentricchia's protagonist is the
anti-hero par excellence – you can't put him down, either physically or emotionally – whose only equal is Fabio Montale from the
great Marseilles trilogy by Jean-Claude Izzo."
—JOHN R. MacARTHUR, PUBLISHER, *HARPER'S*

Praise for THE EDGE OF NIGHT

"Brutal and uncompromising, brilliant and desperate."
—ROLLING STONE

Praise for JOHNNY CRITELLI and THE KNIFEMEN

"Scenes are somber or funny or lose-your-lunch ugly…The sabo-
tage and sadness are real, and the language out of the streets and
kitchens and bedrooms is obscenely authentic."
—ENTERTAINMENT WEEKLY

THE ACCIDENTAL
PALLBEARER

Jan-17, 2013

to Melissa,

Every good wish,

Frank

FICTION BY FRANK LENTRICCHIA

FRANK LENTRICCHIA

THE ACCIDENTAL PALLBEARER

 MELVILLE HOUSE
BROOKLYN · LONDON

 MELVILLE
INTERNATIONAL
CRIME

THE ACCIDENTAL PALLBEARER
© 2013 Frank Lentricchia
Lyrics from "Mrs. Robinson" are copyright © 1968 Paul Simon
Used by permission of the Publisher: Paul Simon Music

First Melville House printing: December 2012

Melville House Publishing
145 Plymouth Street
Brooklyn, NY 11201

www.mhpbooks.com

ISBN: 978-1-61219-171-3

Manufactured in the United States of America
1 2 3 4 5 6 7 8 9 10

Library of Congress Cataloging-in-Publication Data

Lentricchia, Frank.
  The Accidental Pallbearer / Frank Lentricchia. -- First Edition.
    pages cm
  ISBN 978-1-61219-171-3
  1. Friendship--Fiction. 2. Police officer--Fiction. 3. Law enforcement--Fic-
tion. 4. Organized crime--Fiction. 5. Murder--Investigation--Fiction. I. Title.
  PS3562.E4937A33 2013
  813'.54--dc23
                                        2012041214

For Richard MacBriar

and

Pam Terterian

CHAPTER 1

There they are – two elegantly dressed big men in a half-empty movie theater with a sticky floor – in Troy, New York, nine miles north of Albany – Albany, the asshole of America, a ninety-mile drive south-southeast from Utica, down the Thruway whose right hand lanes in either direction approach Third World conditions. Nine miles up America's hole, Eliot Conte and Antonio Robinson await in Troy the start of the Metropolitan Opera's high-definition live telecast of the Saturday afternoon presentation. They sit there eating sandwiches made by Robinson's startling wife – salami, onions, provolone, spicy mustard. They take turns swigging from a wineskin heavy with expensive Chianti, bought by Conte – a tip of the hat, he called it, to Papa Hemingway and the macho tradition of American literature. Eliot knows his American literature. They both know their opera, like a couple of old homosexuals, lifelong companions – these two heteros who sometimes, deliberately, just to bust balls, in the company of tough and disgusted men who feared to mock them, called each other handsome.

Conte stares right, away from Robinson, seeing nothing as he falls fast inside himself – as his nails, with a will of their own, dig deep into his cuticles. He speaks without affect:

" 'I'll get you through the kids,' Nancy says. 'Mark my words, Eliot, before this is over, I will kill our kids.' "

Robinson with a mouthful, "You go to Ricky's? You get the cookies from Ricky?"

"I will kill our kids."

"The imminent ex-to-be lamenting the imminent loss of your erotic power – nothing more."

Conte, barely audible, staring vacantly ahead: "We were doing it maybe twice a year."

"I have to say my wife would be unhappy at that pace."

"Millicent surely requires more."

"Less."

"So I say to Nancy, how old are you, Nancy? She goes, Okay, Eliot, I get it, you cocksucker. She's younger than me? Huh? She's better-looking than me? *This* is why you're leaving me and the kids? You asshole. I say, She's twelve years older than you. She's forty-one, Nancy, and not as attractive as you, either."

"Wait a minute, Eliot. You tell her you're leaving her for what? A better *person*? Not a better piece of ass? You tell her you're leaving her for some older plain Jane of superior *character*?"

"Who said plain Jane?"

"Basically you had the balls to tell her you were choosing a more vibrant personality, a truly complex mind, a finer sensibility – a woman with an impeccable taste for the performing arts, who would never call you a cocksucker. All the while, Nancy assumes, as anyone with the slightest knowledge of the male gender would assume, that you, Eliot Conte, were flushing her down the toilet for a new and juicy piece who makes your cock explode. And you expected her to *what*? Applaud your admirable *values*?"

Eliot Conte, private investigator, B.A., M.A., UCLA. Antonio Robinson, Eliot's childhood friend, his only friend, who'd been a storied athlete in their high school days at Proctor and then again as a thrilling All-American halfback at Syracuse University – now chief of police of their hometown, Utica, New York. Robinson, the city's cuddly black teddy bear – cuddled even by that dying generation of Italian-American racists who control the city's political structure.

It was, in fact, Eliot's father, eighty-eight-year-old Silvio Conte, a legend across the state and a political king-maker, Silvio "Big Daddy" Conte, owner of the flourishing Utica Prosthetics, who had pulled the strings two years ago to get Robinson appointed Chief. Not out of the goodness of his heart. Much less based on a judgment of professional merit. And not out of fear, either, because Silvio Conte fears no one – this visionary political artist who could spot potential years in advance of its actualization, at which time he would seize it and twist it to his benefit. Hence, Antonio Robinson. Hence, "my special son," Big Daddy had called him from the time his biological son and Antonio were children and Antonio took more meals at the Conte home than at his own. Eliot had never felt like a special son. Eliot understood, as everyone in Utica understood, in the absence of evidence – absence being the proof of truth – that strings had been pulled. How else could Antonio have vaulted year after year over higher-ranked men all the way to the office of Chief? Eliot didn't want the details, Antonio never offered any, and

Eliot was grateful. After all, how clean was Eliot Conte? Hadn't his father – it must have been his father who'd pulled strings on his own behalf when he'd returned from the West Coast? When he'd failed the state examination for a PI license, but a month after receiving the letter telling him he'd failed and could try again in six months, he'd received a second letter from the governor's chief of staff, no less, saying with regret that a mistake had been made and please find enclosed a fully executed license and permit to carry a concealed weapon.

Robinson, picking his teeth with the edge of his ticket, "It's been thirty years you dumped Nancy? What's the point of raking up the past?"

"I was called last night from Laguna Beach, California."

"And?"

"At three A.M."

"Yeah?"

"Three in the morning, Robby."

"Spit it out, Professor."

"They're holding her for questioning."

"For what?"

"The murders of my two daughters."

"You have dark comic talent."

Eliot Conte stares at his friend.

Antonio Robinson drops the wineskin.

"Slaughtered in their sleep."

Robinson cannot speak.

"Do you know what I feel, Robby?"

"Talk to me, El."

"I feel now what I've felt for thirty years about the kids.

Nothing," says Conte, at his cuticles again, needing to feel nothing.

"Nothing?"

"As I walk out the door, she says, When you least expect it, asshole."

Robinson suggests they leave and find a full-service bar "because this is no time for – "

Conte cuts him off, putting his hand on Antonio's arm, "Let's stay and enjoy the performance."

"You're in shock, El. Let's go."

"No. I look forward to the last scene, when Don José plunges his knife into her breast, down to the heart – just after they sing with such ferocious passion that it's impossible, handsome, for me to walk to the car without your assistance." (The two elderly gentlemen sitting two rows behind them, who are hard of hearing, stiffen on "handsome," though not in the right place.) "I anticipate the last scene and already my legs turn to jello."

Robinson stands, brushes crumbs off his pants, spots a nice-sized fragment of provolone snagged by his breast pocket, pops it into his mouth – sucks, chews and swallows, sits again, fumbling in the brown paper bag and extremely irritated, "You go to Ricky's. You have coffee with Ricky. You two cunts bullshit for an hour. And then you forget to buy the fuckin' cookies. Listen: Whether you feel anything or not, or you're repressing or not, you need to put this monster out of her misery. In cold blood."

"I don't do that."

"Not yet."

"You know I don't do that."

"Your UCLA exit, Eliot."

"What about it?"

"Demonstrates potential."

"That wasn't me."

"What they all say. Temporary insanity et cetera."

"That really wasn't me, Robby."

"Who was it, Eliot?… Do her the way she did your kids. As she sleeps. Raise your game to the next level."

"If she did it."

"She did it."

"She's in custody."

"She'll walk. Trust me."

"How can you be so sure, Robby?"

"This is what we know. The worst walk."

"Like me. When I walked out on the kids. When they were babies."

"I didn't hear that. I never heard it. Man, your fuckin' cuticles are bleedin' on your pants. Listen: she walks, then you walk back in, propose marriage, and do the right thing on the first night of your second honeymoon. For twenty years, since you returned from the West Coast, you've been doing good and Utica is the better for it. Speaking of which, this Michael C thing we need to discuss at intermission is much worse than I let on. It's bad, Eliot."

As the gold curtain rises at the Met, Robinson leans over and whispers, "Time to fall in love again."

"Take a look at her, Robby — this Amazonian beauty! This is our Carmen!"

In the hush, one last pull each on the wineskin, then

Robinson leans in again and whispers, "You feel something. This is your problem. It's always been your problem."

————————

At intermission, Robinson returns with an eleven-dollar tub of popcorn to the ill-lit area on the other side of the restrooms to find Conte gone. Ten minutes later, having consumed the tub and licked his fingers, he checks the men's room. No Conte. As he returns to their seats, an usher approaches with a note:

> Tenor not in good voice. Taking train home.
> Will discuss Michael C tonight.
> – EC

Something on the floor. He picks up Conte's BlackBerry and pockets it – with no intention of giving it back.

CHAPTER 2

Three blocks from the Galaxy movie house in Troy, detectives Catherine Cruz (40, fit, good-looking) and Robert Rintrona (58, pudgy, red-faced) drink coffee and eat glazed doughnuts in their unmarked car, in a heavy downpour, when a big man without an umbrella, dressed in a gray pinstriped Armani suit and a tie, takes refuge, soaked to the skin, in a filthy telephone booth without a door, a few feet from where they sit. The big man attempts a phone call, then assaults the phone with his forearms, in impotent rage. Too late to save them: His kids are lost. An avalanche of coins pours down onto the floor of the booth and spills out onto the pavement. Cruz, junior partner and driver, starts to get out of the car when Rintrona says, "Forget it, Katie, this is not in my job description. Call a cruiser. They love this shit." She replies, "I'm warning you, Bobby, don't eat the rest of my doughnut," as she leaves the car and flashes the badge beneath the lapel of her black leather jacket. The big man turns meekly around, she cuffs him and they take him, as they say in all the cop shows, downtown – to a windowless room of foetid air, where Cruz and Rintrona sit, she intrigued, he irate, as the big man, who has identified himself as Eliot Conte, tries to explain why he, so expensively dressed, would be walking in a heavy rain without an umbrella, in a neighborhood of dubious character. Rintrona asks if he's "another one of these drug dealers stationed in the Bronx who's come up here to ply your filthy wares. No? The governor's pimp? A homo looking to exploit a Negro child of the ghetto?"

Conte – weary, phlegmatic, not giving a damn if they throw him in a cell for the night or for thirty years – presses softly to his face a towel – how fragrant it is – lent to him by Catherine Cruz. From her locker. He says, "I was trying to call a cab. To take me to the Albany train station. Because I'd lost my BlackBerry. When the phone eats my last quarters, I lose control. I tend to lose control."

Rintrona pounds the table, "That's the fourth fuckin' time you said that, Mister. You lost your BlackBerry? He lost his BlackBerry. Did you check your ass? This is twenty-first-century fuckin' Troy, New York, where there are no functioning telephone booths, as if you didn't know, buster."

"Mr. Conte," Cruz says, "you should be more forthcoming. You give us, sir, the impression that you're withholding."

"Don't you just love my partner's sweet fuckin' civility? Perhaps you would enjoy a cup of coffee, Mr. Conte?"

"Sure."

"You can't have it."

"I'll pay the damages, Detective."

"Why would anyone not from here, dressed like you, come to this shithole?"

"Wouldn't you like to call your attorney, Mr. Conte?"

"I came for the opera. I don't want a lawyer."

"Code, Katie. Opera is code."

"Mr. Conte," Cruz says, with more than professional interest, "would you be referring to the live telecast of *Carmen* at the Galaxy?"

"Yes."

"They do drug deals there, they did a shooting there, he tells me opera. What's your occupation, Conte?"

"Private investigator."

"You motherfuckers are all alike."

"*Carmen*, Mr. Conte, unless I am mistaken, won't let out for another three hours. You came all the way from Utica only to leave after the first act? Doesn't add up."

"The tenor was not in good voice."

"You just say something against Pavarotti, you three-dollar bill?"

"It wasn't Pavarotti, Bobby. It couldn't have been Pavarotti."

"Why the hell not?"

"Pavarotti is dead."

"BULLSHIT!!"

"He's dead, Bobby."

"Whose side you on, Katie? I saw the son of a bitch on television last night. He shaved off his beard, okay? Lost a lot of poundage. Must have had plastic deception done to the face. The guy looked good, younger than ever, and don't tell me, Conte, the voice was not in. The voice was in deep. So much so I felt like I was being ... forget about it, what I felt, it's private."

The smallest trace of a smile appears and disappears on Conte's face. Rough-edged Rintrona is definitely kin.

"I caught that show, Bobby. He didn't have the beard and was a lot lighter, a real stud, who definitely looked a lot younger. Know why? That was a film from 1967."

Long silence.

"Pavarotti is dead, Katie?"

"He's dead, Bobby."

"Shit."

Long silence.

"The son of a bitch sang last night in a way that communicated a lot of beautiful pain to yours truly."

"The agony of the guilty man, Detective Rintrona," Conte says. "The sinner praying to God without hope."

"Why the fuck does he pray if he doesn't have hope, wise guy?"

"Bobby," Cruz says, "it was the Verdi Requiem."

"Who died?"

"Doesn't matter anymore who, Detective. Only the lyric ravishment of the voice matters, the hot flood of sensuous sound lapping us all over, which I agree was deeply in, as you so perfectly put it."

"Shall we drop this faggot talk?"

"Mr. Conte, is there anyone who could verify your presence at the Galaxy?"

"Yes. Antonio Robinson."

"He drove you from Utica, Mr. Conte?"

"Two guys, Katie, who go together to the opera?"

"But, Bobby, that's all you ever play in the car."

"Don't insinuate against my sexuality, Katie. We go over to the Galaxy, that fuckin' garbage dump, how do we pick this fairy out?"

"The only black man, aside from the usher. He's Utica's chief of police. Six foot three, 230 pounds."

"The opera. The chief of police. My ass. Next you'll tell me your father is Silvio Conte, the biggest bastard of upstate New York, bar none."

"He's my father and also the other thing you said."

"Six-three, 230? Huh? This so-called Robinson is you except for the color factor... make a call to Utica, sweetie, and verify the father is the father."

When Cruz returns, she takes Rintrona aside, who blanches. Rintrona turns to Conte, "I am a flawed person, God knows very well how flawed. We'll take you to Albany, all is forgiven both sides."

Rintrona sits in the back with Conte to discuss Pavarotti's guilt, which Rintrona believes to be personal and not an expression of Verdi's sacred music – "because the man who sings this agony of guilt, Eliot – if I may call you Eliot – he lives the pain, he'll always live the fuckin' pain."

Conte says, "Yes, Detective." Then tells Rintrona that Pavarotti left his wife, who was his high school sweetheart, and two daughters in the middle '90s for another woman.

"He left his babies?"

"At the time he was singing the Requiem you saw the other night, they were babies. But when he left his wife the kids were in their thirties."

Rintrona, *con grande passione*: "Man to man, Eliot: He loves his high school sweetheart, and so forth, adores the kids, so forth, but for unknown reasons in 1967 the seed of restlessness stirs in the groinal area, which is also the guilt area. Once those babies achieve their thirties they're not all that lovable, take it from me. And neither is the high school sweetheart. Forget the high school sweetheart! Then the seed has no choice but to burst out!"

"But your kids make such a fuss over you, Bobby."

"The point, Katie, as if you didn't know, I make no fuss over *them*. I desisted years ago. Katie wouldn't look twice at us, Eliot. What a shame. You married by any chance?"

"Was."

"Intelligent man here, Katie."

"Kids?"

"Formerly."

"FORMERLY!" Laughter out of control giving way to a coughing, phlegm-disgorging fit. "This is a man, partner, who can handle the give and take of life. FORMERLY!" Laughing, coughing, hawking up into a handkerchief. "Here we are and here's my card. Anything I can do, hey! you never know, don't hesitate. I'd be honored to lend assistance within so-called legal limits."

Cruz says, "Who, by the way, was the tenor today who wasn't in good voice?"

"Roberto Alagna."

"Kind of dreamy, though not in Luciano's vocal class."

Conte thinks she's kind of dreamy.

"Eliot," Rintrona asks, softly, plaintively, "Confirm something for me, will ya?"

"I'll try."

"Is my partner busting my balls as usual, or is the King of the High Cs dead?"

"Pavarotti is dead."

"Since fuckin' when?"

"September the 6ᵗʰ, 2004."

"WHAT?!"

"Yes."

"Where the fuck have I been?"

 Eliot and Cruz exchange a look and bite their tongues.

"I don't like it, Eliot."

"Detective, neither do I."

CHAPTER 3

He boards the train in Albany at twilight, in a downpour that will not cease for three days. The milk train, they'd referred to it in his youth, which covers the ninety miles to Utica in three hours and twelve minutes. He contemplates his image in the window's filthy glass – the rain-matted hair, the rain-styled bangs. Frankenstein's Monster. Darkness and heavy bags under the eyes. Conte has been an insomniac since his undergraduate days.

Across the aisle from him, a Caucasian male, his wife, his child – fifteen months old. Younger than Conte's when he left them. In the row in front of the little family, a black man, ancient and feigning deep sleep, daydreaming of striking out Willie Mays with the bases loaded. The ancient black man won't stir for three hours and twelve minutes. Several rows beyond, a Muslim woman, veiled, motionless. She'll remain motionless throughout what will ensue. At the other end of the car, a smiling teenage girl, eyes closed, in a Yankees cap, swaying in her seat and aurally shielded from what will ensue by a headset blasting misogynistic rap into her brain. Across from the teenager, a Mexican immigrant who, in about an hour, will beg the Virgin to protect the innocent, that they may come unto her. There are no other witnesses. There are no witnesses. "This car Utica only, folks. Utica only."

The baby begins to cry, full-throated, with piercing tone, as the train pulls out of Albany. The man (the husband, the father) slaps the baby across the face. His wife offers the baby her spectacular breast, but the baby will not suck – it prefers to cry – and when the woman is slow to cover herself the man slaps her, hard on the ear. The baby cries. The daddy slaps twice. Pinches and twists as he pinches the baby's chubby thigh. The baby cries.

Conte, in flight, recalls a televised interview with Pavarotti in which the tenor says that proper breathing technique can be learned by any singer who can execute, while singing, what he does daily, pushing down in a bowel movement. In a lightning-quick non sequitor, the sexy, thirty-something interviewer asks Pavarotti what he does mid-aria if he needs to clear his throat. I do nothing. Nothing? I do nothing because I do not sing from the throat. Like a baby produces the voice, I sing. Are you understanding? Even when the baby cries for ten hours without stopping, no soreness of the throat. *Perché*? Because the baby produces the voice from here, darling, supported from here, below, where the true voice is born. He puts his hand on the interviewer's diaphragm in illustration. It slips lower. (She suppresses the urge, she'll wait until after the interview, to ask him if her true voice is born in her vagina.) When we grow we lose nature. We talk and sing dangerous, from the throat. Pavarotti places his huge hand on her warm throat, his pinky drifting down and finding her breast. I have career like atomic bomb. *Perché*? Because Luciano big baby. Luciano is nature. *Capisci, mia figa stretta*?!

The daddy slaps the baby very hard, three times, on the face. Conte, unable to escape, glances over at the man, who catches his glance and responds with a glare and the middle finger. Conte is afraid. Conte is a timid man. He gives the man the thumbs-up sign and says, "I don't blame you, not in the least."

The rumble of the train in motion and the crying and slapping fill the car like white noise and Conte is seized by the moment that had earned him his expulsion from UCLA, when he'd felt taken over, when he'd become a vessel for rage, when he'd dangled the provost, all five feet four of him, by the ankles out of the provost's fifth-floor office window. "By the heels, like Mussolini in Milan," he'd whispered over and over again. ("That wasn't me, Robby." "Who was it, pal?")

Conte feels himself stand and loom over the man. Feels an enormous belch rising. Leans over the man and lets it all out, all odiferous of salami, onions, mustard, provolone, and red wine. The baby stops crying. The man is startled by the hulk before him, by the stench. The man quickly recovers the balls, which for the moment are still brass, and says, as the provost had said thirty years before, in response to a perfectly reasonable request, "You're a joke."

Conte hears his voice say, "Your son is the next Pavarotti."

"It's a girl. Scram, you ugly fuck."

His voice says, softly, "Are you contradicting me?"

"It's a girl, asshole. This is a fuckin' girl."

His voice says, "Do you know the movie, *Throw Papa from the Train*?"

Conte notices welts on the baby's face, black-and-blue marks on its arms and legs.

The man says, "Get lost."

The man is being lifted out of his seat by the throat. The man is kicking wildly – one kick catches his wife on the side of her head. He's being choked. Choked screams fading. The Caucasian male is dying. Conte releases him. The man drops down into his seat. Conte hears a voice say, "Encourage your son to nurture his vocal technique. Bobby Rintrona will pay dearly to hear him sing. Do you know Bobby?" The Caucasian male loses control of his sphincter muscle.

Conte returns to his seat. The baby wails. The woman bleeds from the ear. Conte dozes. In Utica, he follows the man to his car, a late-model BMW. Jots down the license plate number and, standing in the pouring rain, drenched again to the bone, says, "What is your son's name?"

As he walks away, Conte finds in his hand a ham sandwich that he'd purchased at the Albany station. Tosses it on a sewer cover, where it's promptly swarmed by three large rats.

CHAPTER 4

He boards the bus he still thinks of as the Dago Special –
rides it along Bleecker deep into the formerly 95-percent-
Italian-American East Side, gets off at Wetmore and walks
a block up the rise, in the rain, toward 1318 Mary and the
sole bungalow – "the bung hole," according to Robinson –
Conte's house on a street of well-maintained two-and three-
family structures. Many old Italians of the third generation
remain, but it's a new East Side of immigrants from Bosnia
and Mexico and a sprinkling of deluded adventurers from
Utica's black neighborhoods, who are suffered not. The lights
are on. E. CONTE, says the sign on the front door, PRIVATE
INVESTIGATOR/PRIVATE AFFAIRS.

He opens the door to find Robinson, who's had a key
for twenty years, sitting at the desk in the front room with a
copy of *Moby-Dick* in his lap. Robinson grins and says, "Call
me Antonio." Conte stares, says nothing. The office is lined
with books – city telephone books and directories, going
back twenty years, a few pertaining to the criminal code,
2,000 pertaining to American literature and scholarly com-
mentaries thereupon. The house, beautifully re-done, was
purchased for him, mortgage-free, by his father when he

returned from the West Coast, broke. Top to bottom, in and out, renovated by city workers on weekends at no cost to Eliot or, of course, to his father – the high-end kitchen a gift from local merchants.

"You look like shit," Robinson says. "Not to mention nuts."

"Thank you. I need a hot shower. Then I need seven drinks. In the meanwhile, run this plate for me."

Twenty minutes later, he returns in sweat pants and sweatshirt, hair slicked back, with a big bowl of ice and a bottle of Johnnie Walker Black.

"Where does he live, Robby?"

"You know where Michael C lives. We've been to his parties, how many times? You harbored love for his wife, think I don't know? Still hot for Denise, Eliot?"

"The license you ran. Where does he live?"

"Something happen on the train?"

Conte says nothing.

"You're pretty riled up."

"Where does he live?"

"Close by. Fifteen-minute walk. Next to the florist at Rutger and Culver. His name is Jed Kinter."

"Why is the name familiar?"

"Reports on minor sports. Utica Curling Club. Skeet Shooters of Oneida County. Little League. A glorified gofer at age thirty-five. What's the story?"

When Conte is finished telling him, Robinson says, "Yet another Eliot specialty. Some bastard does despicable things who the law has little chance of stopping until it's too late. So Eliot the Good steps up, a defender of the weak and innocent.

Listen: This Michael C thing takes precedence. Concentrate on *that* and forget Kinter. I strongly urge you."

Conte dumps his ice, pours four fingers of the Johnnie Walker, chugs it, pours another and chugs half, stares hard at Robinson, then says, "Remember after you cut and slashed through the defense for five touchdowns in the championship game, in the cold rain and mud? What were we? Sixteen years old? Silvio cheered until he was hoarse."

After a long pause, Robinson replies, softly, looking away, "I remember the clock ran out and they lifted me up on their shoulders."

"They lifted you high, Robby. They really did."

"The coach took us out for shakes and burgers."

"Silvio took me home. (Long pause.) I say in the car, stupidly, Dad, you never cheer me. How come? He says, You're not a boy for sports. You're a boy for the books. What do you want from me, son? Want me to watch you read *Moby-Dick*? At what point do I cheer? We get home, he asks if I want a cup of hot chocolate. I refuse. He makes it anyway as he hums 'April in Paris.' Pours it in my favorite cup, still humming, smiling to himself. No doubt thinking of your heroics on the field. He puts the cup on the table. I pick it up and pour it down the toilet. We didn't talk for days."

"Man, you know I – "

"It's all in the past." Conte knocks back his drink.

"So what's so urgent about your boorish assistant chief," Conte says, "that you need to drag me in?"

Robinson calculates. The time is not yet right. He'll crouch awhile in the weeds.

"Let's knock back some more of this fine Johnnie Walker,

FRANK LENTRICCHIA

El. By the way, that tenor you walked out on got warmed up after intermission. Alagna, man, the fucker can sing. The two of them made me forget the world. I think I came twice. Fuckin' world, am I right, brother?"

Robinson laughs. He smells blood in the water.

"This is what I'm telling you, El. Kill the guy up on Rutger, kill the ex, kill Michael C and a lot of innocent people are avenged."

Conte suddenly looks alive: "Alagna after intermission was hot?"

"Listen, Eliot, sooner or later, just once, you need to ice someone, to get it out of your system. Rid the world of some toxic waste. Do the worst thing possible, Thou shalt not kill, do the very worst and liberate yourself from all the ways all these years you've been pretending to be someone you're not, and just like that" – snaps his fingers – "all the false Eliots disappear. You feel lighter. You float down the street in your expensive loafers. A clotheshorse like you finally gets to enjoy his clothes, and you never again have to ask yourself who you really are, because you know. Definitively. Guess who's singing in the *Bohème* next week? Alvarez! Can we possibly wait?"

They've had this conversation a million times. Since they were kids. They're both having a good time now.

"You won't kill a mosquito perched on your arm, Robby. Kill her, kill him – annihilate the cunt! You're absurd."

"I never said annihilate the c-word."

"If not you, who?"

"That word I don't use. It was you, Eliot. In your mind you said it to yourself concerning the bitch on the West Coast. Nancy is the c-word."

Robinson winks.

They toast each other, friend to dear friend, taking alternate lines:

Acqua fresca
Vino puro,
Figa stretta,
Cazzo duro!

"In their thirties, your kids are living at home with the ex?"

"Yes."

"Why?"

"Think about it, Robby."

They're on their third scotch on empty stomachs, in the re-modeled kitchen – the most expensive appliances, granite counters, a floor of earthy-beautiful Spanish tiles, Eliot making Italian omelettes and bacon, but no coffee.

"We have four more blasts each of the Johnnie," Eliot says, "who needs coffee?"

"Three is my limit."

"So you don't use the c-word, Robby. So you won't join me on Johnnie four through seven. You're giving me a headache. You're always – you know what it is? You're always: *Listen, Eliot.* For as long as I've known you: *Listen, Eliot.* Me. Not you. *I* have to ice somebody. Jesus, I'm dizzy... Remember that time? Pour me another, handsome. What were we? Twelve? How you cried nonstop, abjectly, when that mangy feral cat killed and ate the baby robin? Eliot! Kill the fuckin' cat! You! The kid everyone feared at school, though you never lifted a finger against anyone. Not even against Del'Altro, Utica's bully-in-chief, who you could've taken out in two seconds and he knew it, two seconds, but he knew you wouldn't because you're a pussy. He taunts and he taunts and you walk away when everyone wanted you to clean Del'Altro's clock. When was that? Junior year at Proctor? By the way, it's not Alvarez in the *Bohème*. Why can't you keep these singers straight?"

"Who is it, El?"

"Probably not Pavarotti."

Conte laughs. Table-pounding hilarity.

"What's so funny? I'm still in mourning. You're drunk, man."

"Somebody new. Young. Glorious tone. Outrageously attractive guy who refers to himself in the third person as Vittorio Grigolo. But the gestures! The guy has gestures – totally ridiculous. Redefines over the top."

"So why drive all that way to witness this embarrassment?"

"Next week, here, Robby, we do what we always do when we listen to the radio broadcast. We cook, but we don't listen to the radio. We play Luciano's recording with Freni and eat *Ossobuco alla Milanese* with a side of *Risotto alla Toscana* and cannoli from Ricky Castellano."

Silence while they contemplate multiple pleasures.

"You have vocal illusions, Eliot?"

"Don't you?"

"With your bass voice, you'd sound like a rapist on the prowl. Speaking of which – " he breaks off. The time is not yet right. Linger longer in the weeds.

"Who cares, Robby? Because I love my illusions."

In the midst of the meal, enough bacon to induce a massive heart attack, and Eliot on Johnnie Walker number six, when Robinson says, "Consider this."

"You're supposed to say: *Listen, Eliot.*"

"Kiss my – the man on the train? Mr. Do-Good? Have you considered that you maybe made it worse for the baby and the wife? Have you thought of that?"

"Shut up, Robby."

Long silence. Conte is wondering how a glorified gofer affords a late-model BMW.

"Right now what's going on in the guy's home? His fuckin' *castle*? Have you thought of that? Maybe the humiliation leads to a catastrophic spike in rage. Is the baby still alive? Or alive but now in addition to the welts and the black-and-blue marks, a broken arm and cigarette burns on the as-yet-uneviscerated torso? And the big busted wife, what is he doing with her body? Has it crossed your advanced mind?"

"Write an opera. You have the talent."

"I've seen everything, my years on the force."

Conte smashes his glass against the tiled floor, then passes out, head on plate in the half-eaten omelette. The phone is ringing. Not the one in the kitchen, but the business phone. Robinson goes into the office, sits at the desk, and listens as the answering machine clicks on:

Hello, Mr. Conte, my name is Ralph Norwald, don't erase me, sir, I am not calling on behalf of Bank of America, but on behalf of your... uh... my wife, Nancy Norwald, the former Nancy Conte. I am

calling you, Mr. Conte, to dispel any thoughts you
may have entertained, though "entertained" is not
the proper word in such circumstances, is it? concerning the call you received in the wee hours of
the morning Eastern Standard Time. That call was
not a cruel hoax. Cruel, yes. Hoax, no. This caller
who made this call was making this call from the Laguna Beach police station out here in Laguna Beach,
California, where you once resided with our wife.
You may well ask yourself, Who made this call? Who
was this male caller who made this call? In truth, it
was a public defender for Orange County, California, who neglected to identify who he is, who is not
an impostor, if you're entertaining that idea, which
if you want to quell further paranoiac ideation all
you need do is check the online editions of the *Los
Angeles Times* and the *Santa Ana Register* to certify
that our mutual wife is being held without bail for
the murders of the daughters you fathered in your
youth and hers, in her. Nancy wants you to know
that they are real, these deaths, and that she is innocent as the driven… uh… the driven Santa Ana
winds, despite the copious blood and brain matter
on her nightgown, in which she greeted the police
at our door. In subsequent online editions you will
learn that Nancy has stated openly and without fear
to the authorities that when she and I retired to bed,
she, as is the custom, because it is her job, not mine,
it was never mine, to turn on the alarm system, she
turned it on, but when we arose the next morning

we found it strangely turned off and the front door unlocked. No signs of forced entry into the home or into… uh… and we certainly heard no screams from bludgeonings in the night because we were stoned on certain brownies, a Nancy specialty, which we consumed in foolish portions before retirement to bed, as we openly confessed to the police because what do we have to hide concerning these deaths, Mr. Conte? I am calling to plead with you via Nancy on her behalf because she will eventually via her attorney request a character-witness statement from you in person at the trial. Speaking of her attorney, though we are extremely rich due to my plumbing practice, Nancy insists, though I think her foolish in her bullheadedness, that she be defended by a public defender to show that she has nothing to hide by having a lousy lawyer. She has a point there. Kindly send me an e-mail and we can go from there. Norwald at excite dot com. We are all in mourning, Mr. Conte, together in this. My awkward articulation to you cannot convey our deepest feelings. When do words ever?

Robinson returns to the kitchen to find Conte still passed out. Shakes him. Nothing. Shakes him harder. He's awake. Robinson sits him up, picks gently from his hair fragments of omelette, applies a cold washcloth to his face and hair, hauls him to his feet, guides him to the bedroom, and says, "Better pee first, man."

"Doan need to."

"At fifty-five, we always need to."

Robinson guides him to the bathroom. Exits. Conte pulls down his sweatpants and pees half in the bowl, half on himself. Removes his bepissed sweatpants and emerges from the bathroom stumbling to bed, nude from the waist down. Says, "I wan' my sleeping medisaytion."

"No. It's dangerous on top of all that booze."

"Give me you mean."

"No."

"I wan' see man in the castle. Talk 'em out of it shoot 'em."

"Goodnight, buddy. We'll talk in the morning."

"I wan' my –" and he's out.

Robinson pulls up the covers, tucks him in, turns off the lights, and on the way out picks up the copy of *Moby-Dick* and locks the door behind him. One of the new Bosnians out walking his pit bull, not recognizing the chief, thinks, Let them stay where they belong. Good to have a bad dog around the black element.

Robinson is beginning to feel the onset of panic. A plan will have to be discussed to take Michael C out of play. Heavy rain. Weirdly, at this latitude, in late October, a rumble of distant rolling thunder. Tomorrow, Antonio Robinson springs from the weeds.

CHAPTER 5

Three hours after his only friend tucks him in, Eliot Conte hurtles from black oblivion to hyper awareness. He switches on the bedside lamp. Sits shivering in the dark on the edge of the bed in a flickering light. 1:30. They always end this way, his ritual Saturday-night binges – with a violent onset of consciousness, booze-dehydrated, in the grip of tyrannous thought. With longing, head in hands, Conte groans as involuntary memory retrieves Catherine Cruz's towel pressed softly to his face, but its seductive fragrance is lost – he needs it back now – the Cruz bouquet beyond memory's grasp. They too were lost? Emily and Rosalind? They were dead? He wants to press Catherine Cruz softly to his face.

Shuffles in slippers and robe to the kitchen where he swallows in one long pull a tall, cold glass of orange juice, eats a handful of potato chips, puts on the coffee, then returns to the refrigerator and stares in, looking for something. Lasagna, three days old. Nausea surges up into his throat. Strides off to the bathroom, removes his robe, quickly tossing it to the floor behind him, and kneels vomiting hard into the toilet – substantial heaves concluding with indescribable shapes bobbing afloat in the darkened water. He gazes in a long while before flushing. Washes face with cold water, brushes teeth twice, shuffles back into the kitchen. Pointless to return to bed because sleep will not catch him until dawn. Remembers and wishes he could honor his paternal immigrant grandfather's self-lacerating curse: "If only I could vomit the poison of myself! *Porca Madonna!*"

At his desk now, sipping a mug of espresso sweetened with two splashes of anisette and fixated in his stupor on the flashing light of his answering machine. Conte is about to play the recorded message when he hears it, a cry – it wasn't in his mind, it had to come from outside – the high pitched rhythmic chant of a soldier at boot camp in a drilled march. *Hut! Hut! HutHut! Hut! HutHut!* Goes to the front window to see him approaching the pool of light cast by the street lamp, in a slow jog, in the rain, the man known in Utica as The Runner, who twice daily – at mid-morning and again in mid-afternoon – cruises Utica's neighborhoods, rich and poor and in between, in jogs estimated to be each an hour long, though no one could say for sure, because who could have cared enough to follow and time him? Seven days a week and yet he's no rail-like specimen of those who train for marathons. The Runner is stocky, average height, African-American, late forties (a Caucasian's clueless guess). Speculation had it that he was a psychological casualty from Gulf War I.

The observant Uticans gossip, Do you know him? No. Do you know his name? No. Do you know anyone who knows him? No. Where does he live? No idea. The Runner was more gossiped about than Silvio Conte. *Hut!* Eliot, who was home more often than not during working hours, has never heard or seen him on Mary Street. Why now at this hour? *Hut!* The Runner has been spotted twelve months a year through withering heat and knifing cold, over snow and ice, but in this monsoon? *Hut! Hut! HutHut!* as he moves through the pool of light beneath the street lamp opposite Conte's house and while passing turns to look at the back-lit hulk in the window as he, The Runner, raises both arms high in a grand gesture of greeting to the man in the window – "*Good mawnin'!*" Conte is hailed! He feels an almost irresistible impulse to bolt out there in slippers and robe and join The Runner – chanting with him through Utica's rain-slick nighttime streets, chanting shoulder to shoulder with a mystery.

Returns to his desk, sits, then rises immediately, ignoring the flashing light in order to consult each of his city directories and phone books, they go back twenty years, the year of his Utica return. Jed Kinter. Phone number, address. Rents the second floor apartment of the house adjacent to Castellano's Artistic Flowers with Elizabeth Kinter and their child, Mary Louise. Tom Castellano is proprietor of the shop and also owner of the house where the three Kinters live and where Castellano occupies the first floor. Three different addresses: the current for three years, the earliest fifteen years back. No record of a Jed Kinter in the oldest phone books and directories. Until three years ago, Kinter lived alone.

Conte dials the number at 2:35 A.M. After several rings, the answering machine picks up. Conte hangs up. Calls again at 2:40, several rings, hangs up. On his third call at 2:45 an angry male answers, cursing, only to hear a familiar, soft voice say: "I know who you are. I know where you live. Keep your son Mary Louise safe and have a nice day."

To the kitchen, a second cup of espresso, anisette again, but in a heavier dose, then back to the desk, hits play button and listens, statue-like. Saves the message, opens his laptop and finds the *Los Angeles Times*, takes notes, then the *Santa Ana Register* for the ugly version. No hoax. Listens to the message again, takes notes. Walks to the window facing the street, this back-lit hulk now weeping and shuddering for the first time in thirty years – not since he'd wept, also alone, as he drove away from his babies and wife for good.

Conte believes his ex to be innocent of these crimes. He couldn't say why. The name Ralph Norwald – out of the past from his UCLA days, he and Nancy newly married, but recalls nothing more than that. This Norwald sounded a bit mental. On the other hand, he thinks, that's what talking to an answering machine might do to a normal person. Doesn't really know if they can subpoena him for character testimony. If they can, he'll fight it.

Pacing, tries to retrieve the image of Catherine Cruz. Hopeless. He can only weep. Cannot distract himself. 3:50. Will not attend the funeral for Emily and Rosalind. Crawls into bed, not bothering to remove slippers and robe. Broods until 5:35 on himself, the person he least wants to think about, or be with.

Four hours later, Eliot Conte is pulled up, slowly this time, from peaceful sleep and a pleasant dream of Detective Cruz, by the insistent ringing of his doorbell.

CHAPTER 6

Conte opens the door to find Robinson with a bag of groceries and the answer to a question that Conte has not yet asked but is about to ask: "Would I use my key when I knew you'd be drunk asleep with that fuckin' .357 Magnum in your bedside-table drawer?"

"Come in, Robby."

"Brains blown all over the walls et cetera."

"Good morning, Robby."

Robinson sets the groceries on the kitchen counter as Conte sits in despair. Robinson says, "You need to eat bland after last night. Very bland. Now get off your ass, sad sack, and put on the coffee while I do the rest, like the mother you've been missing ever since you were eight. Cheer up, El, I'm here."

"Okay, Robby."

"Saw your father as usual for our Sunday brunch at Uncle Henry's. How a guy looks that good at that age is a fuckin' mystery. I mean, he's fuckin' inhuman. This waitress, early fifties tops, was definitely thinking it over. Actually writes her phone number on the bill. The old guy got a kick out of it. He's irresistible on several levels, as Utica, not to mention Albany, has known for several decades. Irresistible except to the son."

Conte sips coffee, doesn't respond.

"Silvio could pass as your slightly older brother."

Conte stares into his cup.

"This morning, the way you look, your younger brother."

Conte puts his cup down, says, "Maybe he could try passing as my father. He should give it a shot."

"That's ridiculous. You bite the hand that feeds."

"You certainly don't."

"You bet I don't. Unlike you, I never had a real father – whoever, wherever the hell he is, he couldn't shine Silvio's shoes."

"Do you shine my father's shoes, Robby?"

"I'll let that one go, because if I don't…"

"Or do you shine each other's shoes?"

Robinson places before his friend two eggs, sunny side up, cream of wheat and apple sauce. Conte rises, the aromas are too much, rushes to the bathroom and mainly dry heaves. Hears Robinson shout out, "What you get for that smart mouth of yours." Conte returns, eats the cream of wheat, leaves the rest. Saying what a fuckin' shame, too bad I already put away a big brunch, Robinson finishes off the eggs and the applesauce, then goes to the cupboard, returns with two slices of bread, salts and peppers the yolk residue, mops it up, all the while never so much as giving a glance at Conte across the table.

"Shall we change the subject, El?"

"When have we ever? Silvio Silvio Silvio."

"For once join me and your father at the 11:00 High Mass."

"No."

"For his sake. Make him happy."

"No."

"Silvio passes the basket during the Offertory. Silvio dispenses communion elbow-to-elbow with Father Gustavo. He's your father, El. He loves you."

"My father who art not yet in Heaven."

"Man, you're a stone killer."

"Good politics, Robby. That's all it is, a religious show."

"Your father *believes*, man."

"In himself alone."

"You believe, El?"

"No."

"I believe, El."

"No you don't."

"Shall we change the subject, El?"

"Silvio Silvio Silvio."

"Did you listen to the call from the coast?"

"Same as you did."

"You were awake while I listened?"

"No."

"How do you know I listened?"

"You said 'the coast.'"

"Eliot Conte, Private Eye. Yeah."

"A five-year-old would've picked up the clue."

"When are you going out there to spill her blood?"

"Get real."

"No urge to avenge your daughters?"

"Get real."

"You're letting this cunt get away with it?"

"She didn't do it."

"You know this?"

"Yes."

"You can't know this."

Conte says nothing.

"You're letting her off, but you're hot to go after this perfect stranger? This Kinter?"

"Yes."

"What can you do to stop Kinter and ensure the child's and wife's safety? Only one thing I can think of."

From out of the pouring rain, *Hut! HutHut!* Conte goes to the window. The Runner stops in front of the house. Black, broad-brimmed, rain-repellent hat. White T-shirt. Red running shorts. White running shoes. He points to Eliot, then to himself. Repeats the gesture. Smiles. *Hut!* and moves on. *HutHut!* Conte returns to the kitchen.

Robinson wants to know, "What's so fascinating about that fuckin' whack job?"

"I think he wants to communicate."

"I think you're still bombed, bro."

"I think he wants to communicate with me."

Robinson is hyper-alert: "About what? Why would he want to communicate with you? For what reason? Are you trying to tell me something?"

Conte says he needs to revive himself with a shower and shave and asks Robinson to lock the door when he leaves for Saint Anthony. Robinson replies, "I'll still be here unless you take more than forty-five minutes to do your fuckin' ablutions." ("Ablutions" induces Eliot's first full grin in weeks.) Robinson goes to the front room, picks up one of the numerous high-end clothing catalogues, sits in the cushy reclining chair slowly thumbing the pages of Bullock & Jones of San Francisco, noting articles he'd seen to advantage on Conte's generous frame and jealous of his friend's ability to pay such prices – Robinson's own elegance of dress an imitation, one-third-price-knock-off of Eliot's. Fuckin' Eliot with his mortgage-free house, peanuts real-estate taxes, thanks no doubt to Big Daddy... drives an eight-year-old Toyota Camry, does his own laundry, does well enough in his private-dick practice to support his sartorial excesses and the opera CDs, his only entertainment expense. No girlfriend to blow his money on. Madame Hand and Her Five Fair Daughters. Eliot, you bitch... Who went for the high-tech surveillance devices? Obviously Silvio. And what does Silvio get in return for his investment of fatherly love? Eliot, you fuckin' ingrate. And me with a spoiled wife and five kids who don't want to grow up. And this fuckin' Michael C who will destroy everything I've got.

Conte appears and Robinson says, "I have to leave in five minutes and you have to listen to me. We have a problem with a serial rape crisis in this town and my assistant chief – that's right, Michael Coca – he's the one. The women will not bring charges and no one knows exactly how many except Coca. Just one, one brave one confided in my wife, who confided in me, and now I confide in you. The victims are all married to my patrolmen, who don't know the story, because the wives have been told by Coca that their husbands in this fuckin' economy will lose their jobs, because Coca sits ex-officio chair of internal affairs and will bring their husbands down regardless they were never out of line. Tells them he wants to dip his wick on a regular basis. Coca will never be brought to normal justice. In other words, El, this is your type criminal specialty. I have no evidence. He uses condoms. No victims who will come forward. My hands are tied. Even Silvio's hands are tied, God forbid it ever comes to his attention with his fragile heart. On what basis do I say serial? Something the one who confided in my wife said he said during the act. Let's talk more if you want to, I can't miss Mass. I have to go now. See you later. You do what you do — I don't need to know your methods. Only Coca needs to know. Me, I'm not even curious whatsoever. El, I'm realistic. Hear me out. No one here is talking about icing anyone, *capeesh*? But Coca needs to have the fear of Our fuckin' Lord rammed hard up his ass. Speaking of which, I don't want to be late for Mass. This is my sincere hope: Five days from now we listen to *Bohème* without this misery hanging over our heads. You're looking a lot better, by the way. Almost handsome." He winks. "See you later."

CHAPTER 7

Robinson shuts the door – Conte goes to his desk to make notes on the serial rapist story and sees immediately that it hangs on the credibility of a single point – that one of the victims actually spoke to the wife of the chief of police, in spite of Coca's threat, and that Coca, in the act, in cold passion, told this woman in so many words that he was victimizing other wives of police officers. Conte considers three theories. The so-called victim who spoke with Millicent Robinson is Coca's cast-aside secret lover, eager for revenge. Or Robinson has made it up because he wants Conte for some reason to inject such fear into Coca that he, Michael C, will be rendered harmless. The first theory required Conte to believe that Coca was stepping out on his wife, when all public sightings suggested that after many years of marriage Coca was still (unfortunately) besotted with Denise. The second theory required Conte to believe that Coca posed a life-altering threat to Robinson. Conte wanted to believe the first, hell hath no fuckin' fury like a woman scorned, because it might give him a chance with Denise, were she lost in an unhappy marriage. But he could not believe it. The third theory: There's a hidden darkness in Michael Coca and Conte's best friend has not lied to him.

Antonio Robinson will be at Saint Anthony for another hour and then repair to the rectory with Silvio Conte for their Sunday coffee with Father Gustavo. Eliot can count on perhaps two hours alone with Millicent Robinson. If the second theory is correct, she would need to sustain under indirect probings a believable lie.

The Robinsons live in a freshly painted ranch-style house of the 1960s – clapboards in white, shutters in high-gloss black – on Deerfield Hill in north Utica. A hint of the Adirondacks beyond. It's an area of well-kept and not-so-well-kept single-family dwellings, where the neighbors allow their dogs to run and shit freely; where actual deer devour gardens and shrubs and the nice people keep on planting them; where raccoons pry open tightly closed garbage bins, take up residence, and have cute families in a number of vulnerable attics in the not-so-well-maintained houses, whose clapboards at the roof line are rotted; where the Robinsons are regarded as the neighborhood's great good fortune, a black bulwark against creeping lower-class black and Hispanic crime and falling home values because he's the big-shot head cop and he paints his house every two years, doesn't he? Where everyone – the comfortable and those clinging to the bottom edge of the middle class – have sweeping views of the wicked city spread out below.

Millicent Robinson greets him at the door. Slim, lovely, with dramatic cheekbones, small breasts (big enough to fill one's mouth) and a smile that would melt the heart of the most hardened racist. She says (but where is it, that shattering smile?), "Hello, stranger. Tony told me you'd be coming to see me today at this time."

Conte is tongue-tied, red-faced.

She says, "I've made sandwiches in anticipation. Coffee? Tea? Or me?" She laughs the laugh of a person with a much bigger body. Deep, room-filling. "How are things down on Mary Street? The minorities having their day at last?"

Conte replies with a hug and "Hi, Millicent. Thanks. I'll take a sandwich and herbal tea if you have it." He hasn't seen her in a while. Follows her into the dining room where two places have already been set and a bag of ginger-twist tea – his favorite – already sits in an empty cup against which leans a three-by-five index card printed upon in big block letters: ELIOT. He thinks, Am I already in over my head? Am I already drowning?

She puts on his plate a tuna salad sandwich in the Italian style – olive oil, onions, capers, spicy Sicilian olives – and pours boiling water into his cup. A half sandwich, a glass of red wine for herself. She says, "For Tony, I had to learn to cook Italian 24/7 or he wouldn't have married me. My husband is ethnically confused. Or is the word 'deluded'? Periodically I remind him he married a coal-black woman." She raises her glass: "*Salute! Paesan!*"

Seeing no point in small talk, he says, "Robby" – she's never called her husband that – "told me a shocking story this morning and I wanted to get your take as I move forward."

"How long ago was it Tony secured that retainer for you at Hotel Utica? Eight years is it? When he became deputy chief? My, how time flies. They still send you a monthly check for your unique services?"

"They do."

"You run background on their employees?"

"I do."

"Nail employee thieves, that sort of thing, Eliot?"

"Yes."

"Tony swears by you."

"As I swear by him."

"I believe he swears by you more than he swears by me."

Conte croons softly and low:

"And here's to you Mrs. Robinson!
Jesus loves you more than you will know,
Wo! Wo! Wo!"

"Why, Eliot Conte, you have a nice voice. Less white, I'd say, than those boys who made that song. I'd say that over the years you and Tony cross-colorized each other. By the way, do they alert you at the hotel when the cheating spouses of the upper crust meet their lovers there?"

"Yes."

"Isn't that how you put the photographic screws to Judge Carmore? Whose wife, thanks to you, put major screws into the judge in the divorce settlement, which he quickly agreed to lest your dirty pictures hit the internet?"

No response.

"Then she committed suicide anyway with those dirty pictures no doubt in her mind of the judge giving head to her sister?"

No response.

"How you get pictures like that is beyond me. Shall we eat these wonderful sandwiches? You don't look well, Eliot."

"I'm starved."

"Tony tells me the hotel sets aside a few remote rooms which you've already technically primed for your pornography. They send the adulterers to those rooms? That a fact?"

"Yes."

"Forgive me, Eliot. Seems like I've forgotten that it's you who's supposed to be asking the questions."

They eat in silence, she nibbling, he wolfing, and when they're finished she brings out a fresh teabag for him, takes a second glass of the *vino* and says, "I'm so pleased that you want to help Tony and these poor violated women. Tony tells me you don't have a girlfriend yet. Going through life that way – "

"I met someone in Troy yesterday."

"I'm so happy for you."

"I'm working up the courage to call her. Her name is Catherine Cruz."

"Let's cut the bullshit, shall we, sweetheart?"

"I'm here to gather information, Milly. I'm sorry."

"Don't call me Milly. That's what Tony calls me when he thinks it's about time, finally, to play hide the big salami. That's how you Italian people talk, I believe. Hide the big salami."

"Sorry."

"You're a big fella yourself." (There's that smile!) "Fire away."

"When did this woman talk to you?"

"Day before you and Tony went to the opera. Friday."

"Morning? Afternoon? Evening?"

"Ten in the morning, exactly, Detective Conte. My, you are detailed!"

"You remember the time *exactly*, Mrs. Robinson?"

Sparring. Round one.

"I was leaving for a 10:45 appointment with my hairstylist when she rang the bell."

"No point in asking you her name."

"None."

"It would help."

"Justice done to Coca without mercy would help."

"What precisely did she say that indicated to you that she was one of a series of rape victims?"

"If I were white you'd see me blush. He told her she had the tightest one so far on the force. There have been others and there will be others, I'd guess he hopes with even tighter ones. He's looking forward to the future."

"Tightest which?"

"Please, Eliot."

"How old is she?"

"Young. Early thirties, I'd say. Three little ones."

"Three kids? How tight can it be?"

"You'd be surprised, sweetie. I've had five. They stitch you up tighter than it was when you were inexperienced. Made Tony happy. Back in the day. These days only his work makes him happy."

"Where did it occur, the alleged rape?"

"Try not to talk like a son of a bitch, Eliot. Alleged. There were vaginal abrasions. Visible."

"You saw them?"

"Do you suddenly not understand 'visible'?"

"It occurred where?"

"At home."

"Where were the children?"

"In school, I presume, except for the four-year-old, who pounded the whole time on the bedroom door."

"And the newborn?"

"She never said anything about a newborn. Where'd you get that thought?"

"Seems that's what Robby told me. Who I presume heard it from you."

"I told him no such thing. I don't like your assumptions, Eliot. As if I had some hidden agenda in all of this. Trying to trip me up as if I were some kind of – "

"I'm sorry."

"About what?"

"The skeptical impression I'm giving you. It's just what I do."

"Take everyone as concealing?"

"Most everyone."

"She said she was humiliated by him."

"Did she spell it out?"

"No."

"He has anal proclivities, you know, Millicent."

"How would I know? Or you, for that matter?"

"That's why we called Michael Coca ever since the eighth grade Michael *Caca*. As we grew older we grew merciful and called him Michael C. He understood the reference."

"He is shit."

"Do you know Denise?"

"Very well."

"Did she ever indicate anything of an unusual sort, girl to girl, concerning his proclivities?"

"No, and what the devil does this – "

"Did he rape her anally?"

She looks away, pained.

"You have beautiful hair, Millicent."

"Why thank you, handsome."

"I bet Ann Iacovella does your hair. They say there's no one in Ann's class in this town."

"I don't have white hair, Detective. You come here to talk about my hair?"

"Sorry. I'd rather talk about your lovely appearance than rape. Can you blame me?"

"You know how to talk to a girl, Eliot. Give my husband some pointers."

"Why do you suppose she came to you? I mean, given the threat against her husband?"

"I have to tell you, hon', she danced with the bastard at the Labor Day Ball. That comes out, a lawyer will insinuate from that. Tear her apart. I wouldn't be surprised if he danced with all his victims."

"He dance with you?"

"He did, but he didn't fuck me."

"He came to her house in broad daylight?"

"And in uniform."

"Shrewd. If he's spotted, it's official business in a neighbor's mind. What do you and Robby want me to do, Millicent?"

"Stop him."

"How?"

"I heard from Tony that you have a way with bastards."

"He exaggerates."

"How did you get that pederastic minister to leave the state?"

"Showed him a picture."

"Tony said you made David Del'Altro leave Utica. The teenage bully, wasn't he, who kept on bullying into his late forties when, thanks to you, he moved to Akron? According to what they say. You have stature, Eliot. I can't imagine Akron."

"Robby exaggerates."

"Among those who know these things, you are regarded with awe. Other people say other things. People, you know, trying to get at the questionable father by calumniating the good son. In my opinion."

No response.

"Tony said you did something, but you wouldn't tell him what. You just giggled. Give Milly the details, sweetheart."

"True, Del'Altro beat up kids in grade school, high school, even at Utica College and on into his thirties and forties he'd physically intimidate co-workers at the post office. This is well known. In a small town, everything is well-known. Nothing actionable, you understand. Can you arrest or sue someone who shoves an elbow into your ribs in close quarters? Or spits on your pants? When he hurt the small father of a small boy, I made a plan."

"What did he do to the small father?"

"Broke his jaw. No witnesses."

"What did the father do to incite Del'Altro?"

"Not a damn thing."

"Can it be?"

"I know Del'Altro. I've known him since grade school, when he hurt little girls. I know what I know."

"How did you find out about the incident?"

"The small boy tells his friends who tell their parents et cetera. I went to the father to verify the grape vine. In front of the son, it was done, the broken jaw."

"Then springs the noble Eliot into action!"

"The first thing I ... He doesn't have a garage. Just a car-port. In the middle of the night, I affix a personalized plate over the front bumper. The way the car is parked, he'd get into it the next morning without passing the front. Per-sonalized. You've seen them. His said, I, FAGGOT. He drives around for a couple of days, so I gather, in ignorance. Pass-ing vehicles blow their horns. Teenage boys yell out, 'SUCK ON THIS!' Then, at the post office, one of his fellow clerks, much meaner than Del'Altro, much bigger, says to him, 'You decided it was time to advertise it? You finally coming out of the closet?' Del'Altro says, 'What?!' The guy says 'Keep one thing in mind, Dave. I will not, no matter how much you need it, I will never fuck you in the ass.' Del'Altro takes a swing at him, the guy knocks six teeth out of Del'Altro's head. Made him look like a carved-up Halloween pumpkin. Two days after this incident, middle of the night, I screw a long screw into one of his tires, tight, then reverse a couple of turns. Slow leak. The next day he leaves work to find a flat tire. I repeat the procedure three times, a different tire each time, over the next ten days. Del'Altro becomes increasingly hostile at work to the customers. Tells one, who complained about the price of first-class postage, a woman in her late eighties, to go fuck herself. To her credit, it is said that she replied, "Would that I could, because you could never satisfy a real woman like me." He's suspended without pay for a week. One morning during the suspension period he walks out of his house in heavy fog and steps down into a substantial mound of human feces. I let a month go by. The middle of the night, I pour a two-gallon container of bleach into his gas tank. You've heard the stories of sugar in the fuel line? Pure urban myth. Bleach is the real deal, Milly. The next day, three quarters of the way to Rochester, the car simply stops. Sixty-five miles per hour then nothing. The engine is destroyed beyond repair on his new Buick. Takes the bus back to Utica. Two weeks later he's driving a two-year-old Ford Fiesta. I bleach again and tell an investigator friend of mine for his insurance company that Del'Altro is a well-known scammer from way back. He goes to Del'Altro's house – this got into the *Observer-Dispatch* – he questions the claim and Del'Altro, now nearing insanity, decks him. Del'Altro is arrested, gets six months in the county jail. Upon release he moves to Akron."

"Bravo, Detective Conte!"

"Milly, had Robby done a number on him when we were at Proctor High, Del'Altro – he may have turned out a decent citizen and even, who knows, a good man."

"Violence can be a cure?"

"Sometimes we reach that point."

"What do you have in mind for Michael Coca? Akron, too?"

"Milly, I'm going to send him to the bottom of hell."

Back home, Conte immediately contacts the owners of Utica's three African-American beauty salons and tells each that he'd like to buy a $200 gift certificate for their most well-known customer.

The first one says, "Who would that be, darlin'?"

"Millicent Robinson, who had an appointment with you day before yesterday. Friday at 10:45."

"Never heard of any Millicent whatever."

The second responds, "That stuck-up oreo bitch never set her ass in my shop."

The third responds, "Let me check my book. Oh yeah, she comes here, but she had no appointment at 10:45 on Friday. She had her hair done two weeks ago on a Monday at 4:30."

"Do me a favor?"

"I don't cut white hair. That's beyond me."

"Keep the gift certificate a secret until her birthday, which is in three weeks."

"My lips are sealed. Be sure to put that check in the mail now – real soon, dear."

CHAPTER 8

Conte's arm feels like a 500-pound boulder as he places the phone back into its cradle. Goes to the kitchen, pours a very large Johnnie Walker on the rocks and carries it to the front window where he stares, glass in hand, at the rain that has thickened again – wind-driven now in a mean slant against the house. The Robinsons had lied. He hasn't touched his drink when he abruptly returns to the kitchen – pours the Johnnie Walker into the sink – leans over low and inhales the rising odor of expensive scotch.

He'd always known Millicent Robinson as a woman of subtle indirection, but she'd made it almost crudely clear. After all my Italophilic husband has done for you, whether you believe our story or not, you owe us and let's not ever pretend you ride a white horse. Add Coca to the filth you swim in. Do it for Tony, if you love him.

Michael C is not a rapist, he's convinced, but then what exactly has he done to make himself so threatening to the Robinsons that Antonio wouldn't reveal it to his brother-in-all-but-blood, whom he'd asked to take Coca "out of play"? Whatever that means. How had he put it before going off to High Mass? Ram the fear of Our fuckin' Lord hard up his ass. Whatever that means. Should he confront Antonio? Or play along?

For Eliot Conte, time seems never to pass or (greatest of all blessings) disappear, except at the opera. (Sex too, formerly.) His practice consists mainly of repetitively sordid cases of adultery. Of background checks that rarely turn up anything surprising. Of runaway kids he sometimes locates and retrieves, but mostly doesn't. Of hours of butt-numbing surveillance, sitting in his car, pissing in an empty coffee cup, drumming his fingers on the steering wheel and, if he's lucky, at the end of it all, snapping a compromising picture with a telephoto lens. So much for doing good for Utica.

He'll play along, why not, and maybe become the lead character, the tragically flawed but essentially decent guy, as he fancies himself, in a story whose end lay hidden, like those time-killing Scandinavian detective thrillers he'd been reading lately one after another as fast as he could. The very sorts of novels that the author of a UCLA Master's thesis on Melville and Faulkner used to scorn – well-wrought pulp, elegant trash, and altogether mind-blowing (like the opera always, like sex once was) and a total cure while the books lasted. The treacherous hard stuff that he abuses, usually alone on Saturday nights, in order to obliterate time and thought, only hurls him deeper into depression and the dead time of boredom that seems never to pass.

They would play him for a fool. Okay. He'll play the fool. Meanwhile, on yet another lonely, time-crawling Sunday afternoon, Jed Kinter awaits his attention.

He's leaning low over the sink – hoping futilely for a buzz in the brain.

Castellano's Artistic Flowers, at the corner of Rutger and Culver, has a front entrance on Rutger and a side entrance on Culver. The two-family house where Castellano occupies the first floor and the Kinters the second is just around the corner on Culver. Conte calls ahead and tells Castellano that he'd like to meet him at the shop.

Castellano says, "It's Sunday, for God sakes. Come to the house."

Conte responds, "Do me the favor of meeting me at the shop."

Castellano says, "I'll see you at the side entrance."

Conte responds, "Indulge me, Tom. I need to come to the front entrance."

"Quick, Eliot," Castellano ushers him to the back room, "because I don't want people to formulate ideas that on a Sunday – coffee?"

"No, thank you."

"I'll pour you one anyway, just in case."

"Okay, Tom."

"Have one of these," Castellano pushing a plate of six biscotti before him. Conte takes one, but doesn't eat.

"So hush-hush, Eliot, like a private dick, you're here all of a sudden after how many years? You should know I personally made those biscotti. They don't come from Ricky's. My so-called brother."

Tom Castellano had been Conte's first case twenty years back. He'd just married when his wife, the former Candace Bowles, started to step out on him four days after the honeymoon – in the open at the most popular restaurants and bars. When Castellano confronts her, she tells him, "No problem, I get half the shop regardless." Artistic Flowers was Utica's most lucrative and had been Tom's grandfather's and father's pride.

So Conte shows her a photo. She yells, "You're crazy, I never did that. You somehow created that disgusting picture." Conte replies in his characteristic soft monotone, "Yes, I did, and I'm going to nail it to every telephone pole in this town and mail one to your blueblood father unless you legally renounce your rights in the shop." She says, "I'll sue." He says, "A lawyer acquaintance of mine will see you tomorrow with the proper documents, lacking only your signature. Keep in mind, Candace, that a psychiatrist, who happens to be an acquaintance, at the proceedings – should it come to that – will recommend Marcy State Hospital for what this photo shows. Marcy State, Candace." She makes a last attempt: "You want a blowjob, Conte? Is that what this is all about?" Tom had said to Conte at the outset, "I'm not a fag, you know. Because I know what they say about me as a flower person. Believe you me, I got her good on the honeymoon, every which way. I even used devices."

She renounces, they're quietly divorced, but the grapevine was intense for months and Castellano's humiliation was beyond description and repair. Conte stayed away because he didn't want to be yet another reminder, and he never told Tom how he'd convinced his wife to be reasonable – never showed him what it pleased Eliot to think of as "ocular proof."

Conte takes a bite out of the biscotto, dunks it in the coffee, and finishes it off. Takes another one. Same routine.

Castellano says, "Good, huh?"

"They are. They really are."

"So what's the story, Eliot?"

"Your next-door tenants."

"You're kidding."

"Ever hear any screaming coming from the apartment? Constant baby crying? Like last night?"

"Screaming? You serious? You're shitting me, right? The baby cries, they all do, though I don't have any first-hand experience, thanks to that cunt I should've killed with my bare hands. Constant crying? No. You're thinking spousal abuse?"

"I presume you checked with his previous landlord before he signed the lease."

"Everything was up to snuff. I called down to the paper, by the way. No problems there, either."

"There was a landlord previous to that, too."

"News to me, Eliot."

"See anything out of the ordinary last night or this morning?"

"Definitely. Last night on TBS I saw *Psycho* for the first time."

"Nice, Tom."

"I have to confess, when she gets stabbed in the shower? I got turned on. I wanted to fuck Janet when she was getting stabbed. Especially then. I was almost hard. Tell me the truth, Eliot. How abnormal am I?"

"My guess is that many men share your feelings."

"Including yourself?"

"Anything is possible."

It crosses Conte's mind that Candace Bowles may have had her reasons.

"He took out the garbage last night, pretty late. That out of the ordinary?"

"Does he usually take out the garbage late at night?"

"Sometimes. Don't we all?"

"Nothing of interest to tell me?"

"Come to think, he took the garbage out again this morning. A little odd, no?"

"Do you always wear your hearing aid, Tom?"

"Not always. I put this fuckin' thing in your ear, you'll find out."

"Did you wear it last night watching *Psycho*?"

"Never when I watch TV. I turn up the volume. Okay, I get your drift."

"Kinter complains about the volume?"

"No. He's an ideal renter."

"How loud, Tom?"

"Loud. Maybe I wouldn't have heard anything, okay, which I doubt there was anything to hear."

"In the house, you never wear it?"

"I live alone. What's the point?"

"Do me a favor. Knock on the door – see if anyone responds."

"And if they do, then what?"

"You're a shrewd guy. Invent something."

"Hey! I saw *Rear Window*."

"Nice, Tom."

"Only because I owe you big time, Eliot." He leaves and

when he returns, "No one home unless there's a corpse up there. In case you're wondering, I knocked very obnoxiously many times. Jesus Christ, Eliot, you're pretty extreme."

"Okay. Call."

Castellano calls. The answering machine.

Conte takes another biscotto.

"Tom," chewing, "I need to borrow your key to their apartment."

"That's an illegal act, as if you didn't know."

"Not if you put the key in and come in with me."

Conte knocks heavily and repeatedly for thirty seconds. Nothing. They enter. Walk around. Nothing remarkable. Conte inspects the bathroom with care. The tub. Asks Castellano to fetch a screwdriver. Castellano throws up his hands, "*Madon'*, Eliot!" When he returns with the screwdriver, Conte opens the tub's strainer, puts his finger in, and circles it around. Clean. Takes a wooden spoon from the kitchen, wraps its long handle with tissue paper, which he secures with the vaginal lubricant he finds in the medicine cabinet, inserts in the drain and twists it around. Pulls it out. Nothing. Thinks, Kinter could have run hot water a long time. Or maybe used one of those powerful chemicals that clear drains.

Castellano says, "What's it all about, Alfie?"

"I'm looking for blood and tissue."

"Christ, these are normal people."

Technicians from the police would need to get into the trap, but there is no reasonable cause for suspicion that a crime has been committed, unless Antonio would do him a favor. Bone fragments? Teeth? In the trap? Conte says, "Let's check the garbage cans."

"We should've checked those first before looking for evidence of a slaughter. If we're talking crazy."

Downstairs, at the cans, "Those are my bags," removing the lids, "and his real big ones I don't see and neither do you, Sherlock." Castellano adds that he saw Kinter head to the backyard that morning, but his view doesn't permit him a sight of the garbage cans and even if it did he doesn't make it a habit to watch his tenant throw out the garbage.

Conte says, "Maybe he put the bags in his car. Does he park back here?"

"My aching balls!"

"Can you see his car from your back window?"

"You mean my rear window?" Laughs. "Just the front. The angle is off to see the trunk. You're thinking chopped-off body parts, stuffed in garbage bags, that were stuffed in the trunk, which the car is not here, so he disposed somewhere, for Chrissakes? You know this Jed Kinter? Is that it? You wanted to come in the front entrance of the shop because you don't want to be seen from his apartment? Is that it? That why?"

"Yes, to all your questions."

"You on one of these new medications or something?"

"You're an interesting man, Tom. Does he have a storage place?"

"The attic."

Conte looks for suitcases. Finds only one. It bears Kinter's identification tag. He says, "Thanks for your time, Tom. Do me one more favor, please."

"You're insatiable."

"Say nothing to anyone about my visit, including your brother Ricky."

"Ricky doesn't talk to me anymore."

"Very sorry to hear that."

"On one condition. You tell me now how you persuaded my ex."

"Fair enough. I showed her a color picture of herself on all fours with a dog. The dog's fire-engine-red penis is in full evidence, ready for action. The dog's tongue hangs out. There are suspiciously colored smears on her cheeks. Her tongue is buried in the dog's ass."

Extended silence.

"What type of dog?"

"A Chihuahua – named Lyle."

Extended silence.

They return to the shop's back room.

The coffee. The biscotti.

Castellano finally speaks. His voice atremble. "Tell me you doctored that thing. Tell me it never happened. My judgment with her was off. Granted. Tell me it wasn't *that* off."

"The photo is authentic. Unbeknownst to you, you married a dangerously sick woman, capable of anything. Thank God, Tom, you didn't have children with her."

"Thank God," Castellano making the sign of the cross. "Don't be a stranger, Eliot. Come over once in a while for coffee."

"I promise, and if you think of anything, no matter how trivial it may seem, call me immediately. May I take the rest of the biscotti?"

The light is flashing on Conte's answering machine. Hits play: You have two new messages. First message, left today at 2:16 P.M.

> El, Robby. Turn on your fuckin' cell. Your father expressed heavy sadness in the company of Father Gustavo that he rarely sees you. Father Gustavo recommended patience, but Silvio is really up there in the years. What else can I say? I'd like to see you in the next day or two concerning you know what. Call me.

Second message, left today at 3:26 P.M.

> Hello, Eliot. This is Joan Whittier. You may remember me as Joan Dearborn, a long time ago. Our kids used to have play dates at each other's houses. I read about what happened in Laguna Beach and I am so sorry... oh, God... this is terribly awkward. I have information for you that came to light a month ago when Christine, my daughter... do you recall her? She's been in therapy for many years, can't hold down a job, and has struggled with an eating disorder... it came out that... you may remember that Bunny and Ralph Norwald had daughters we all occasionally exchanged play dates with? Ralph sometimes babysat. Christine had a memory of Ralph, she says he molested her when she was at his house to play

with Cindy and Judy Norwald. I don't put much stock in this recovered-memory idea, but it made me remember that once when I was going to take Chrissy to the Norwalds' she balked and kicked out a window in our apartment. Another time she bit me so hard she drew blood. I don't know what to say except I know that after he divorced Bunny, Ralph married Nancy when your girls were quite young. I also know that Chrissy was in touch with your girls in recent years. She says they didn't have jobs and were both bulimic like her and living at home... like Chrissy is. If you want to talk my cell is –

The call is dropped.

He retrieves the number, but doesn't call. Ralph Norwald. A fleeting image. Happy face. Goofy smile. A superficial man... who became rich. Nancy was ignorant of it? She knew and didn't know? She didn't want to know, because she knew?

CHAPTER 9

He leaves a message:

> Robby, El. I'm taking a wild guess your lovely wife
> didn't keep it a secret I stopped in. She made a fine
> lunch and we had a productive conversation. Uh…
> listen, I have a plan to uh… neutralize the party in
> question. Neutralize, shall we say, with prejudice. I'll
> give you a ring tomorrow night or early Tuesday
> morning. Okay, that's it, *paesan*. Stay out of this bibli-
> cal rain.

He thinks about calling Joan Whittier, but can't do it. He'll
never be able to do it. Puts his head down on the desk, just to
close his eyes for a minute or so as he retrieves Joan's image
from thirty years back – long-legged in shorts and movie-star
beautiful, walking a two-year-old hand in hand – then opens
his eyes and it's an hour and fifteen minutes later and he has
a powerful desire for a blast of his drug of choice. Conte
feels it's time to switch off for a while, cut back to something
lighter in impact. Beer, cold beer. He used to drink a lot of
beer in college and even more in graduate school. No beer
in the house.

On the way to purchase a Czech import, Conte considers alternatives for the meal he'll make. It's one of his chief
pleasures, maybe number one on his life list, to envision meals
to come. In detail. Driving home with twelve bottles of the
Czech beer secured and looking forward to their utilization,
Conte sees spaghetti *al dente* in a sauce of garlic and extra-
virgin olive oil – sees himself not chopping but slicing, actually shaving the garlic with a razor blade into slivers so thin
that they dissolve while sautéing in the hot oil – sees himself
coarsely chopping the parsley, adding it, and sprinkling gen-
erously in at the end crushed red pepper and two pinches of
salt – sees himself leaning over the pan, inhaling – how he
loves the slicing and the chopping, more so even than the
meal itself – and fresh from the crisper a salad of arugula
and chicory to cleanse the palate in preparation for Ricky's
specialty, he'll tackle a double serving of Ricky Castellano's
overwhelming Sicilian cassata… Ricky, the overwhelming
Sicilian.

Kills two bottles while preparing dinner, another with
dinner, and two more to fortify himself for the phone call
he must make to Robert Rintrona because her number was
listed nowhere and the Troy Police Department, as he knew,
would not give it out, though he would ask anyway. He can't
imagine calling Rintrona and opening with, "Detective Rintrona, this is Eliot Conte – I was just wondering if you might
be able to give me Detective Cruz's phone number." Of
course, whatever diversionary prelude he'd invent would be
seen through. At least, though, there'd be a decent delay and
his romantic interest in Catherine Cruz wouldn't immediately be out in the open. A little cover might (might) deter

Rintrona from sardonic retort. And since Rintrona, who was in awe of Silvio Conte, perhaps even in fear of him, had offered Conte assistance, if ever he needed it, he decides to ask him to run a background check on Jed Kinter through the various databases available to him as a law enforcement official, all the way up to the FBI. It couldn't hurt to get the facts, if there were any facts of a criminal sort to get. Antonio Robinson could, of course, do him this favor, but he needed the Chief of Police to believe he was working full-time on Michael Coca. The bitter truth is that he can no longer trust his only friend.

At Rintrona's home, a young woman with a sparkling voice answers and says, "Daddy, it's for you." After the exchange of pleasantries, Conte says, "By the way, there's a pirated Pavarotti recording of *Ballo in Maschera* that I happen to own. It's astonishing – better than the Decca issue."

Rintrona replies, "Are you telling me the fuckin' Bologna *Ballo*?"

Conte says, "Yes, that one, and by the way, I'll be in Albany on business tomorrow morning and maybe I could stop by and loan you my copy, which you could burn if you like."

Rintrona says, "Who do I have to kill?"

Conte laughs, then makes his Jed Kinter move.

Rintrona immediately responds, "Area code 518-555-1212."

Conte says, "What?"

Rintrona says, "She doesn't have a landline. That's her cell. I'll meet you at the Melville Diner, 1303 Front Street in Troy, not that far from the station."

"Named after Herman Melville by any chance?"

"Is there any other fuckin' Melville worth naming anything after? You know, he lived around here for a while, but they didn't preserve anything because the authorities have their heads you know where, I'm trying not to use foul speech for a change. Good luck with Katie, you'll need it. See you at the Melville, shall we say 10:00 tomorrow morning?"

"Sure. Do get me the dope on Jed Kinter, Robert, if you don't mind."

Rintrona's already there when he arrives. The place is empty, shabby, clean. On one wall, an actual harpoon, but his attention is riveted by a large painting, behind the cash register, of a looming white sperm whale in dramatic breach. The whale's formal boundary is everywhere porous, its whiteness spilling into the whiteness of sky and white spray of the burst sea. Something indefinite about the whole, something, something nameless and unimaginable – it attracts him and fills him with fear, like looking over the edge of a high balcony. Throw yourself over.

Rintrona is talking with a sexy waitress in her late forties, whom he pats on the hip as Conte approaches. She says to Conte, "He acts like I'm in love with him since he's been coming here for the last fifteen years – like I think he's too good for me and that I don't have everything I need right at home with Big Paulie, who's very big, you can take it to the bank." Rintrona pipes up, "Big Paulie is the consolation prize, Loretta, let's face it." She says, "What'll you have, handsome?" Conte, in the swing of things, shocks himself: "I'll have whatever Big Paulie most likes having." She looks at Rintrona and says, "This one," pointing at Conte, "is worse than you." They're having a very good time.

She brings him a mug of coffee and an outsized croissant, jelly and butter, and parts with, "Bobby is a softy who spends his entire life covering it up, what a g.d. shame, but I know who you are, darling, don't I?"

Rintrona, blushing, "Let's keep it between the three of us. Don't mention it to Big Paulie."

Conte pushes the CD of *Ballo* across the formica surface. Rintrona pushes a manila folder and says, "You get the worst of this deal, Eliot, but I'm not complaining. Good to see you again. Guess who did it?"

"Who did what?"

"The painting you couldn't take your eyes off of."

"The late great Herman Melville himself?"

"Big Paulie. Hell of a nice guy. I love' em both. When are you seeing her?"

"For lunch."

"Hey, I'm happily married, like Loretta and Paulie, otherwise…"

"Otherwise you'd sweep Detective Cruz off her feet."

"Without saying." Points to the manila folder. "What's your interest in this animal?"

Conte tells the story.

"Once in a while, Eliot, bastards like Kinter meet their match, which almost makes me believe in God, just like that telephone met its match the other day. Who would guess you're a scary guy – the opera, so forth, the gentle demeanor – all of a sudden someone's life is hanging by his fingernails when the opera lover becomes a rage machine. The apple doesn't fall far from the fuckin' tree."

Conte, looking away, "Silvio Silvio Silvio."

"No offense. I never meant to insinuate your father does violence. People in politics fear him, this is well known, after all. He's got their balls in his pocket and periodically squeezes hard to remind them who they are and who he is. Your father's the Lyndon Johnson of New York politics. Me, I was always a big LBJ fan – especially when he made reporters interview him as he sits on the can shitting up a storm. In other words, he welcomed the press into their true element."

Tapping the folder, Conte says, tonelessly, "Why not give me a quick summary of what's in here?"

"At fifteen, he's expelled from high school in Galveston and placed in meaningless detention for assaulting a female teacher."

"Rape?"

"Strictly fists and feet. At sixteen, he takes a baseball bat to a kid's head, who barely survives with permanent brain damage. Charges are mysteriously dropped. Kinter's father is a mover in Texas oil, who's probably the solution to the mystery. At seventeen, he shows up in Philadelphia. According to FBI sources, he becomes a low level gofer for Joseph (The Maximum Ayatollah) Stonato. At eighteen, he shows up in Providence, Rhode Island where he somehow attaches himself to the Patriarca family and becomes a serious person, suspected of being the trigger in two Mob-related executions. At twenty, he moves to Utica, that was fifteen years ago, where I'm sure you know he's been working for the *Observer-Dispatch* ever since. Keeping his nose clean as far as we know. Those are the facts. I can't prove it, but an animal like that doesn't keep his nose clean. Why does he move to Utica? Why would anybody? Something's going on and I don't mean child or spousal abuse."

"I'm grateful, Robert."

"Call me Bobby, what the fuck."

"Let me know what you think of the *Ballo*."

"Definitely. Anything I can do down the road with regard to this piece of work, let me know. I have a personal method for dealing, which doesn't involve the death penalty, which he obviously deserves it, but I don't go that far. Because as an upholder of the so-called law I have actual compunctions. The jury is out on you, Eliot."

"I'm grateful, Bobby."

Conte stands. Gives him his card and tells him his new cell won't be active for a day or so. They shake hands.

Rintrona says, "You didn't touch your croissant."

At the register, Conte winks at Loretta as he puts fifteen dollars on the counter and goes to the door. She calls out, "Handsome, that's way too much for the two of you."

He responds, "So?"

Of course, he had feared that she'd turn him down, but the phone call to Catherine Cruz the day before had gone easily his way. He told her the white lie that he would be in Albany on business and "wondered" (trying hard for casualness) if she'd have time for coffee or lunch. She replied that she'd be working in the squad room all day, but would be happy to join him for lunch on the early side, "if that's convenient for you." When he said that he had no idea about Troy eateries, she laughed gently and replied, "We don't really have eateries in Troy, in the sense I think you mean, Detective — we'd have to go down to Albany for something fancy — but there's a barbecue place I like, if that's okay with you" — anything is okay with Conte — and gives him the address. He was certain that Catherine Cruz had seen through his story. Her tone was cool, but also somehow inviting. The combination excited him. Saying her whole name in his mind, *Catherine Cruz*, excited him.

He arrives at the Q Shack fifteen minutes early, the rain at its heaviest, visibility virtually zero. Under an umbrella that is too small, comically out of proportion to his impressive frame, he walks swiftly from the parking lot, head down, and when he reaches the awning, finds her already there.

"Detective Cruz."

"Detective Conte."

They shake hands. His shyness makes it difficult to keep his gaze focused on her... that face. Her gaze, on the other hand, is unflinching, laser-like, unnerving. No criminal would have a chance. He won't, either.

The Q Shack is a small cinder block building with a shamrock painted on the door, crammed with picnic tables and featuring a long, steaming cafeteria-style counter. Thirty to thirty-five men — hearty, burly, dressed for hard labor — fill all available tables. As they await their turn in line in awkward silence, it crosses Conte's mind, only half facetiously, that Troy, New York, must be the leading edge of America's Gay Liberation movement and the Q Shack its latest All-American expression, a lunch place catering to working class homo-sexuals. The Queer Shack.

He breaks the silence, "A lot of men here, Detective. Aside from you, no women." She tells him that it's a favorite of Troy's plumbers, electricians, carpenters, house painters, and cops. He asks for the meaning of Q. She answers, "Short for barbecue – let's get some Q – not Q for queer, Detective." (*Mind reader.*) She adds, "Don't you think we should call each other by our first names, Detective?"

"A pleasure, Catherine."

"Likewise, Eliot."

"Do you prefer Kate or Catherine?"

"Catherine, though no one calls me that."

"Catherine with a K or C?"

"C."

"It makes a difference in my mind, all the difference in the world, when I hear it with a C, rather than a K."

"Is that a fact, Eliot?"

"Yes, Catherine with a C."

(This kind of flirty banter is a shocking first for Conte.)

It's their turn to order: "Detective Katie Cruz herself!" "Jesus Mary and Joseph! I ain't seen her in two days!" "Kiss me, Kate!" "Who's your great fella there, my Kate?" "Oh, her fella has a mighty presence, he does!" "I don't think he's Irish, Seamus, I don't see it at'all." She replies in the spirit of things, "Sure, and another word outa ya and you are all bound for the slammer."

He orders what she orders: an overflowing pork barbe-cue sandwich, potato salad, and lemonade. The cashier tells him his money is no good in Troy, "It's on the house, lad, because you're the lucky man to be spendin' time with the ravishin' Miss Kitty O'Cruz." Conte's about to say there's no place to sit when the cashier says, "Your place is secured as usual, Kitty," and Conte follows her down a short hall to an office with a desk, a table, and sudden privacy.

They sip their lemonade and before either can start on the sandwiches and potato salad, Conte – unable, unlike Catherine Cruz, to bear the silence – launches a story about his paternal grandparents because the "Q Shack," he says, only half-believing the analogy, "with its male domination brings it to mind."

"Really?" she says, with a twinkle in the eyes.

"Back in the day, Catherine, there once was in Utica an establishment called Donnelly's, and a grand Irish saloon it was, the Q Shack of its time" – warming to the narrative now and sounding like an Irish tale-teller – "where no women were ever allowed."

"Could that have been legal, Eliot?"

"They didn't have the right to vote, so I guess it was. My grandfather was a serious anarchist – "

"A bomb thrower?"

"Metaphorically, and a poet. It was a fine summer night and he was out for a long post-dinner stroll with my grandmother. A ritual of theirs, even in the winter months, and on this particular night their journey took them beyond the east-side Italian ghetto to Utica's central district and Donnelly's, an institution that Umberto had never set foot in and knew not its gender policy. He was a moderate drinker of red wine who rarely partook of the hops, but it was hot and he was thirsty and the prospect of a cold one was irresistible, and so he said to Amelia – the meekest and sweetest of women and a teetotaler – Let us stop here, *cara mia*. And so they entered Donnelly's, where no woman, or Italian, had ever set foot, and all the many men turned and stared, but only briefly because they were gentlemen, despite their Irish hostility to Italian immigrants. Umberto drank his tall cold beer and with his free hand held Amelia's hand and said, in Italian, It is tranquil here. And no one said a word except the waiter, who had taken the order and asked if the lovely Mrs. would like something, too, but the Mrs. required nothing, not even a glass of water. (Long pause.) End of tale. I fear that I made a bollocks of it, Ms. O'Cruz." They're both grinning ear to ear.

"When did they discover they had integrated Donnelly's?"

"Much later. Years."

"Amelia was the anarchist's bomb?"

"Never thought of it that way. Sure. Do you happen to know the saying, You're the bomb? It means – "

"I do know it, Detec – Eliot."

Desperate, casting aside all shyness, and again shocking himself, he says, "I'm too old to play games, Catherine. I confess I have no business in Albany. I couldn't bring myself to say I wanted to drive eighty miles just to see you because I think you're the bomb."

"I believe you just said it, and I never for a moment took your Albany story seriously."

"You knew all along?"

"I did."

"And you – "

"I'm here. Are you?"

"This is unrealistically quick."

"It is."

"Now what?"

"Shall we downshift to first gear?"

"I'm fifty-five and I guess you're about – "

"Forty, exactly, a week ago."

"A belated happy birthday."

"Thank you."

"Our age difference is…"

"Significant."

"Meaning, Catherine?"

"Who knows? Shall we downshift?"

"We really should. This is unrealistic."

"You've been married and divorced, as you told Bobby and me. I can't help asking what you meant by saying that you had children, formerly. Just your dark wit?"

"I couldn't resist the wordplay. You know, formerly married, formerly had children. Actually, I haven't seen my two daughters in twenty years, since I left California and moved back. The alienation is irreversible – and no longer as painful as it used to be."

He excuses himself. Goes to the men's room, splashes cold water on his face. Leans awhile on the sink, shaking. Returns, pulled almost together.

"Are you okay, Eliot?"

"I'm fine, really. And you? Were you ever married?"

"I have a twenty-one-year-old daughter from a very rash, very stupid, and very brief marriage. Twenty-one years ago."

"See her frequently?"

"Not enough for me, but enough for her. I'm mostly grateful for what I have."

"Let's try to eat," he says. He's fairly sure now that he won't break down. "It might be a good thing. To eat."

They do, in a silence magnified many times by the sounds of voices from the dining area, of men who seemed to be riding wave after wave of good feeling. He's thinking that the conversation has hit a wall.

He says, "I wish we had the time to, but you need to get back soon, don't you?"

"I do. Time to what, Eliot?"

"To have a more traditional what-movies-have-you-seen-lately, so-you-like-opera-too type of conversation as a possible..."

"Possibly as a prelude to?"

"You wouldn't mind getting together again?"

"I'd like that."

"Maybe a leisurely dinner, maybe?"

"Why not?"

"I could drive down again."

"I could come up to Utica."

"You'd do that?"

"Yes."

Under umbrellas in the parking lot, he says, "It's supposed to clear up tomorrow."

"So I heard."

"Catherine."

Like the sunshine that would break through the next day, she smiles and says, "Call me or I'll call you."

"I'll call."

"Or I'll call."

"When shall we two meet again?"

She replies, "It doesn't have to be in thunder, lightning, and rain."

"Macbeth," he says. "What a darkness."

She puts her hand on his shoulder. He places his hand over hers for a moment.

He gives her his business card, tells her all information is accurate, though his cell, "as you know... I'll have a new BlackBerry tomorrow."

He watches her walk to her car. Doesn't move until she's driven away.

He's relieved that Catherine (with a "C") hadn't pursued the subject of names – how a Conte, whose grandparents escaped the absolute poverty of southern Italy, with his father in tow, got to be named Eliot. If only he'd been called Anthony or Frank. His mother wanted Richard, but Silvio vetoed "Richard Conte" because it was already taken by a movie star. When his wife offered what she assumed would be the irresistible "Silvio junior," her husband responded that his son deserved a name with "American power," because he was certain that an Italian-American boy armored with "Eliot" would cut a course through to a place barred to a Silvio, a Carmine, a Domenico, a Francesco.

Eliot never told his father about the grade school teasing, or how the heirs of proper Americans at Hamilton College, and later in graduate school at UCLA, called him T.S. Eliot and were eager to inform him that in his case T.S. stood not for the poet's Thomas Stearns but for Tough Shit. So it was that a name no one would link to Silvio's dark world of ethnic politics became the trigger of his son's painful self-consciousness, which he wore like a pair of trousers with suspicious stains at the crotch.

CHAPTER 10

Home from Troy by midafternoon to find a message on his answering machine – it's Robinson:

> You don't pick up on your cell. Or are you really home and listening to this, you pervert? Check e-mail.

He does. Two messages. Rintrona, informing him that he'd played sick and left work to listen to the Bologna *Ballo*, "which surpasses all my sex experiences." The second, from Robinson:

> Have something against turning on your fucking cell? I've got thrilling news from California. Like I predicted, she walked. Your ex was detained for questioning for forty-eight hours and released this morning. No probable cause to charge her for what she obviously did. No arrest. She tells the press that, like O.J., she'll mount a private investigation to bring the real killer to justice. Time for you to lose your mind, El. Speaking of which: neutralize you-know-who before he does more damage to the innocent of this fucked-up town and turn on your cell.

E-mails Rintrona:

I hear that sex can be operatic.

E-mails Robinson:

My cell was lost or stolen. New one by tomorrow or Wed. We need to talk soon re neutralization.

Considers contacting Nancy about Joan Whittier's phone call, but what would be the point? The kids are dead. What good would it do her to learn that Ralph Norwald may have abused them when they were little? If he felt anything at all about the fate of the kids, it was an unacknowledgable relief that they were physically gone, who had been gone for him for so long. Easier to think of them as the kids, rather than Rosalind and Emily, if he had to think of them at all. "The kids," not "my kids."

Before he moved back east, their bi-monthly visitations were occasions of pain beyond his ability to describe. Followed by bone-numbing exhaustion. He'd drive down the 405 from the San Fernando Valley on Saturday morning, a two hour journey to Laguna Beach under good conditions, arrive at 9:00 A.M. to pick them up, only to find Rosalind and Emily hiding deep in closets, under long coats, crying in terror of their daddy's arrival. Or he'd arrive and be met by Nancy in the driveway, who'd tell him their little playmates had asked them over for the day and wouldn't he like to let them have their fun rather than?... If he objected, and knowing he didn't have a pot to piss in, she'd say, "Take me to court, you selfish prick." Nancy had gotten him, as she'd promised, through the kids. From the beginning.

He wanted her dead. Had actually come close to making a phone call to someone he knew was connected, but it was the kids, not Nancy, who were dead, and now he wondered why he shouldn't also be dead. Kill Nancy. Kill yourself. And the miserable little family escapes to a better place, together again at last.

After he'd return them on Sunday afternoons, he'd knock back a few stiff drinks and go to bed, no later than 7:00 P.M., to sleep through without a stir, until seven the next morning. He came to fear visitation weekends. He felt better on the weekends when he wasn't scheduled to see them. After almost ten years of this, as he scraped by on adjunct positions at various community colleges, and unable to write a word of his book on Melville, he made the decision to return to Utica.

Blessedly, the cases of Jed Kinter and Michael C defer thoughts of his children – thoughts that cling, nevertheless, to the cliff edges of his consciousness. And now, since lunch at the Q Shack, the thought of Catherine Cruz was claiming the center, driving out everything else. A thought so vivid it seemed that she herself lived in his mind. A future. A renewal in his life's last phase. A path to sobriety. But she, who he barely knew, was in Troy, and he was in Utica, and he had pressing business to attend to, so much the better to distract him from her absence and all else he needed to be distracted from.

He opens his notebook to the Kinter entry. Why, indeed, had he come to Utica, of all places, fifteen years ago, to lead a so-called normal life? He suddenly decides to straighten out? Get a real job? Marries? Has a child? Was Rintrona right in speculating that Kinter's nose wasn't clean and beneath the child and spousal abuse lay something worse, if anything could be worse than what Eliot had witnessed on the train? Fifteen years ago Kinter had moved from Providence, and the bosom of a notorious crime family, to take up residence at 403 Chestnut Street. A short street, he sees from his much-consulted map of Utica – a few blocks from Oneida Square, on the south side of town, in a neighborhood where Utica's classic ethnic minorities of old – the Italians, the Poles, the Lebanese, east and west Utica primarily – had not penetrated – a quiet neighborhood of small, well-kept one-family dwellings, solidly middle class, in contrast to the two- and three-family structures of east and west Utica, which housed the working class and the lower end of the middle class, neighborhoods not so quiet – noisy, where people gathered on street corners and porches to smoke, argue, gossip, pontificate on the insults of life, and above all to compare notes on the progress in summertime of their backyard gardens – the tomatoes, the lettuce, the cucumbers, the pole beans and the grape vines, where the robins conducted their relentless thievery and shitting and Eliot Conte's best childhood memories had their origin, when he had lingered alone in his father's garden. His notes show that the owner of 403 Chestnut, who lived there fifteen years ago, still does. Sidley McPherson.

He knocks and introduces himself, handing over his card, to a male in his mid-twenties, Sidley McPherson, but clearly not the McPherson he was hoping to question about a former tenant. Young Sidley, seeing his puzzlement, "Junior. You were expecting my father, who passed away six years ago."

"I'm sorry. It was important for me to speak to, uh, perhaps... may I ask if your mother is still alive?"

"You can ask."

"Is your mother alive?"

"She's alive alright."

"May I speak with – "

"At work. Utica College. Department of English executive secretary for years."

"May I ask another question, Sidley?"

"Yeah. Come in." He does not offer Conte a seat, though he himself sits in one of the living room's four soft leather chairs, circa 1975.

"Your home, from my limited perspective, is charming and cozy and – "

"Small. It's small."

"I can't help wondering where you'd put a tenant."

"Is that what you came here to investigate? A tenant? We don't have tenants anymore, but in the good old days they rented out a sexy little apartment above the garage, which is where I live, if you're interested."

Conte turns to the door, "Thank you for your cooperation."

"My cooperation? What is this? Some kind of criminal inquiry? What did the old lady do?"

"As far as I know, Sidley, nothing at all."

"As far as you know?"

He smiles a small smile and leaves.

Eliot Conte had twice taught at the college as an adjunct in continuing education ten years ago — a course in nineteenth-century American fiction. When he walks into Janice McPherson's office,

"Why, Mr. Conte! How nice to see you!"

"You too, Janice."

"You remembered me after all this time!"

"Yes," he lies. "Actually I went to your home and Sidley sent me over. Didn't realize you were still working here."

"How are you, Mr. Conte?"

"Pretty well. You?"

"Just fine, thank you. To what do I owe this delightful surprise?"

"Strictly business, and I'm afraid it has nothing to do with Hawthorne and Melville."

"Oh? Would it be detective work?"

"I'm afraid I'm here in a professional capacity and need to ask you to keep our conversation in strictest confidence, if you wouldn't mind."

Janice feels the thrill of adventure. When did she last? Perhaps she'll help this impressive man pursue a criminal investigation? Be his affectionate sidekick — he looks to her like he could use some affection.

"I fear that I'm interrupting your work, Janice — "

"Not at all. Please come in and sit down."

"Good. I'd like to jog your memory about a tenant you took in fifteen years ago, who stayed with you for eight years, I believe. Jed Kinter."

"Really? Why, he was so quiet. No trouble at all, but I suppose those are the people — what has he done?"

"As far as I know, nothing at all. I'm interested, if you can remember, in the impression he made on you."

"Well, quiet, as I stated. No trouble. Nothing interesting, shall we say, Mr. Conte. Nothing impressive to make an impression." She resists a wink on "interesting." She finds herself suddenly witty and attractive. "He was taking night classes over at Mohawk Valley Community, they must have been journalism classes, because he got that job at the paper. No, that's not right. Come to think of it, he had that job at the paper when he moved in."

"Did you ask for a reference?"

"He gave us a name in Providence, Rhode Island. Please sit, Mr. Conte! A phone number, which I called. A man with an Italian name, I can't remember it, and a cold voice, I remember that, who said that Jed was a serious person, a man of honor, who could be trusted. That was good enough for me. He seemed nice enough and we needed the money at the time because my husband — oh, I won't speak ill of him."

"Did he have visitors?"

"I don't think any except for one, not long after he moved in. I'm sure of the time frame."

"Why is that, Janice?"

"Jed moved in August first in that record heat wave, you recall that, I'm sure. You don't!? Over a hundred degrees every day for sixteen days and the old folks without A/C dropping like flies. How could anyone forget, unless you didn't live around here then?"

"I lived here, but at the time I was in Austria, for the Salzburg Festival. I heard about the terrible heat upon my return around the first of September."

Conte remembers something else about that record hot August. While in Austria, he'd missed the biggest moment in Utica history since George Washington stopped through. Jed Kinter, with his Philadelphia-Providence pedigree, a serious man of honor, the voice had told Janice, was in Utica when the infamous action went down.

"A whole month in Austria listening to the sound of music! The hills are alive and whatnot! How nice for you!"

"It was sublime, Janice."

"What did you enjoy most?"

"They did lots of Mozart and Strauss, which I like well enough, but that production of *Don Carlo* – "

"Verdi's *Don Carlo*?"

"The very, Janice, but if you wouldn't mind, could we get back to that visitor? Forgive my officiousness."

"Of course! Let's follow the scent, Detective! I'll tell you why this visitor was unforgettable. Here it was, one hundred and eight degrees, and he comes out of Jed's apartment dressed in a black suit! That's mentally strange, if you ask me. Did he think, the fool! that black would ward off the sun and heat and humidity? I can see him like it was yesterday."

"Can you describe him?"

"That's easy! I see him in contrast to Jed, who I recall as slight, short and with a very fair complexion, and nice looking in a risky way, whereas this man dressed in black was taller, he had a moustache and heavy black hair, thick, you know, and sort of... he had high hair."

"Italian hair? Is that the idea?"

"You could say that, although your Italian hair is a lot nicer and I'd even say it was – well, Jed, his hair was almost blond and quite fine. No body to it. A woman notices a thing like that. This man had a swarthy complexion and was broader in the shoulders and I'd say a couple of inches taller. My husband's height. White dress shirt, black tie, black shoes. Dark glasses."

"He was leaving?"

"Yes.

"Morning? Afternoon?"

"Morning, I'm sure of it because I'd just finished watering the poor flower garden when he came out."

"Did you speak to him?"

"I said good morning, but he said nothing in reply. No manners, Detective."

"Did you see him arrive?"

"No."

"Did he come back?"

"Not that I know of."

"You never saw him again?"

"Never again."

"Did you notice the car he drove off in?"

"No. It's hard to park on Chestnut. Jed had to park on the street, for instance, but not necessarily in front of the house, unless he was lucky."

"Other visitors over the years he lived with you?"

"As I believe I said, I never saw anyone in the eight years. No women, if that's on your mind. He paid the rent. He was clean. He even raked the yard one autumn when my husband's back went out, which he did without us asking, of course. My husband's back went out a lot, believe me. Not to mention the headaches at bedtime. Jed was the best tenant I ever had. You know what I mean? He paid the rent and it was like he wasn't even there. You can't beat that."

"I hear you, Janice."

"A cup of coffee?"

"I'd love one."

They drink coffee and gossip about the epic intradepartmental feud between Brown and Nathan. When he takes his leave, he gives her his card and says, "You've been very helpful, Janice. If you think of anything at all, no matter how – "

"Oh, I watch all those detective shows! I'll call you immediately, no matter how trivial it may seem! And if you, Detective Conte, can think of something that I might do to assist your inquiry, will you feel free to call me?"

"You can count on it, Janice."

She goes to the door with him. Gives him quite a hug – her body not angled back as women will do, with men other than spouses and lovers, but up close, tight against him.

CHAPTER 11

Conte pulls out of the college's Visitor Parking lot – heads home – anxious, overwhelmed. Until 3:00 A.M. Saturday morning, when he'd been awoken by the call from Laguna Beach, his work had been undemanding – rarely was there ever more than one case on his schedule in any given two-week period. Sometimes none at all. Now, in three days' time, first his children, then Jed Kinter, then Michael C, and pressure, heavy pressure from the Robinsons – then the call from Joan Whittier. And since lunch with Catherine Cruz in Troy, his stomach has suffered an invasion of butterflies.

He makes dinner. A small salad, a grilled cheese sandwich, glass of cold seltzer. (Head over heels: guaranteed weight loss.) His private motto: I can juggle one ball at a time, but only with difficulty.

Kinter's criminal past, as such, is not his major concern. It is the fear that Antonio was not wrong to suggest that his intervention might shove Kinter, his manhood in question, over the edge. Conte feels responsible for the safety of the woman and child. (The flawed but noble Conte.) He wants to do something (but what?) to neutralize Kinter, somehow put him out of play – ram the fear of Our Lord et cetera, so that, what? So that Kinter would forever after become a good father and husband? As if that could be assured, short of killing the man. Who killed his girls? He had a thought, but was on the wrong side of the country to do anything about it. On a whim of overheated speculation fly out to California and kill Ralph Norwald? Assuming it was Norwald. Assuming he could kill anybody, even his daughters' killer.

Conte is a tribalist of southern Italian background for whom loyalty to one's family and friends trumps morality and (goes without saying) the law. He needs to be loyal to Antonio Robinson, all the more so because he had not been loyal to his father. Or to Nancy, Rosalind, and Emily. Never mind the disaster of the marriage. Or the self-absolving rationalization that the kids would be psychologically injured growing up in a loveless house. That they would be better off. If he hadn't left Nancy, wouldn't the kids still be alive? He'll help Antonio in his trouble, whatever it is, he doesn't need to know, but help how? He has no idea what he intended when he told Robinson that he would neutralize Michael C "with prejudice." He hadn't used, because he understood the meaning of the CIA euphemism, "terminate with extreme prejudice." Conte feels certain that he is not capable of killing.

Nibbles at his sandwich with his laptop open, Google-distracted from himself, in search of a story that surely commanded several days of front-page coverage in the *Observer-Dispatch*, about the event that took place while he was away in Austria, fifteen years ago. He'd been told about the heat wave of that August, but only as an afterthought. Because the major topic of conversation all that fall was the most spectacular – theatrical, really – execution in U.S.

Mafia history. The triple assassination of the legendary Albert Aristarco of Staten Island and Frank and Salvatore Barbone, Utica's double representation in the upper echelon of Cosa Nostra – in Utica's oldest Catholic cemetery, at the burial site of Aristarco's godmother, Filomena Santacroce, dead at ninety-six and her nurse thinking, Good riddance to the nastiest bitch I ever attended.

The archived article in the *O.D.* foregrounds the facts that he'd not forgotten. Who could? The shooter was one of the pallbearers, a last-second replacement for one of the official pallbearers, Filomena Santacroce's nephew, Raymond DePellaccio, who suffered a paralyzing lower-back spasm just as the casket was about to be lifted from the hearse and up the steps into Saint Anthony, where Father Gustavo awaited to celebrate the Requiem Mass.

A follow-up account refreshes his memory: heavily enhanced police protection was ordered both for the Mass and the interment. Two police vans, each bearing twenty officers in bulletproof vests and helmets: one for the Church, the other for Calvary Cemetery. The mayor and chief of police at that time, both now dead, presumably of natural causes, were intent on seeing that disaster would not strike in Utica, whose ill repute still lingered from the fifties and sixties – the Sin City of the East, as New York City tabloids had headlined it. The van scheduled for Saint Anthony was in place when the hearse and the cars of the mourners arrived. The van whose officers would form a protective ring at the cemetery around Aristarco and the Barbones – a circle of steel and firepower – never made it because this van, according to three witnesses, had run a red light (a fact vigorously disputed by the police) and broadsided a city bus. Minor injuries for some of the bus riders and eleven policemen, but not the driver, who alone wore a seat belt. Death the consequence of this accident for the three Mafia heavies, each of whom was shot in the head with a small-caliber hand gun. Small caliber, the streetwise reporter had informed his readers, so the discharged round had sufficient force to rattle about inside the brain – up and down and all around – but not enough power to exit. A search for Raymond DePellaccio, the original pallbearer, turns up his obituary: dead several weeks after the shooting, of natural causes.

Description of the substitute pallbearer gives Conte a thrill. Several bystanders at the church and cemetery offer accounts to the police and the press that resemble the description that Janice McPherson had given him of the man she saw on that blazing August morning fifteen years ago. The rude man who refused to return her greeting. Jed Kinter's visitor. If that man and the substitute pallbearer were in fact one and the same, then Bobby Rintrona was right: Kinter hadn't kept his nose clean.

About the murdered Mafiosi, Conte gives not a damn. Let those vile bastards kill one another, it was a police matter that the police shouldn't even bother to investigate. But if Kinter were involved and could truly be implicated and put away, then his baby and wife would be out of harm's way for good, and about that possibility Conte cares too much, like a man who has something to prove.

He manages to eat the salad, but only half the sandwich. Closes his laptop. Nothing to be done until tomorrow, when he'll have to hold off Robinson so that he can pursue a plan of inquiry he's beginning to hatch that will require him to speak to Rudy Synakowski, the reporter who did the original stories, and Enzo Raspante, the photographer, whose photos outside Saint Anthony – picked up by the major news services – had appeared on the front page under the caption: NINETY MINUTES TO LIVE.

He declines the kind invitation from Johnnie Walker – instead packs up his .357 Magnum and spends the next two hours at the police range (a time-killer like the opera) firing 125 rounds with lethal precision into human silhouettes at twenty-five and fifty yards. Then home again to play Joan Whittier's call numerous times, as he makes a transcript. Near midnight, takes the transcript to the twenty-four-hour Fed-Ex – Kinko's station in New Hartford and mails it to Laguna Beach. When the clerk guarantees delivery by Wednesday morning, no later than 10:00, Eliot Conte feels a thrill not unlike what he felt when he examined his fifty-yard target and saw that he'd clustered five shots in the circle marking its heart. Nancy's heart. Norwald's. Kinter's. Michael C's. His own.

CHAPTER 12

Tuesday – sun at last, in a cloudless sky. Conte can't remember when he'd slept so well – eight hours, uninterrupted, deep and no dreams that he can recall. He's sitting at his desk over coffee – showered, shaved, dressed for the day and with no thoughts of Johnnie Walker and about to call Rudy Synakowski – when his doorbell rings. Father Gustavo, who asks if Eliot might spare him a few minutes.

Conte offers coffee, Father Gustavo says he's had his cup for the day, "thank you," but he'll take "orange juice if available, but hold the vodka." A forced chuckle from Father G. Conte does not practice his Catholicism, has not set foot in Saint Anthony since his confirmation at age twelve. After an embarrassing silence at the kitchen table, the nervous Father G says that during his post-Mass meeting on Sunday with Antonio Robinson and Silvio Conte, Antonio had revealed the "enormous tragedy" that had struck Eliot's daughters and "you, yourself."

Conte says nothing.

"Would you like to talk about it, Eliot?"

"No."

"Good."

"Good?"

"This is what they think I'm on earth for. I have other functions, but this is the one they want."

"Grief counseling?"

"I despise the phrase. Grief cannot be counseled. There is no so-called 'closure' for the grief, and you will never 'get on with your life.' The phrase sickens me."

"The language of psychobabble, Father."

"Yes, and the tip of the iceberg in this contemptible age. Your heart is damaged beyond repair. I didn't come here, my —" he suppresses "my son." Father G is ten years Eliot's junior. "I didn't come here to urge you to speak of the unspeakable, about which we should remain silent."

Eliot remains silent. A long pause.

Father G says, "Touché," then adds, "Silvio is distraught, I've never seen him this way. He spoke of seeing the children as infants, when he flew to California as a proud grandfather. His grief is enormous."

"I don't carry vodka, Father, but we do have Johnnie Walker. Would you like a shot? On the rocks with a splash of water? Pure rocks?"

Father G considers. He's not much of a drinker, but wouldn't mind one now. He finds Conte compelling and intimidating. He'd like to win him back to the fold, thinking, absurdly, that if Conte can't be won, then there is little hope for the Church in this terrible country.

Father G says, "I won't push it. Your father tells me you drop in to see him once a month, if that. When was the last time?"

"Don't recall."

"He's at the end of his life."

"I know that."

"He hopes for reconciliation."

"I don't."

"After all that he's – "

"Done for me?"

"You said it."

"What does it prove, Father? Except that he, maybe in guilt, honors the forms of parenthood?"

"But not the spirit?"

"If he did it in guilt, I'd take it as a positive sign."

"Ah. But you accepted his largesse. How do you, if I may ask, grade yourself in the daddy department?"

"Bless me father, for I have sinned."

"And for penance, you awake, do you not, in the middle of the night without the distractions of daylight, to think the thoughts you flee?"

"You said the Requiem Mass for Filomena Santacroce, did you not?"

"I say Requiems all the time. Who was she?"

"Fifteen years ago. On a very special day in Utica history."

Pause.

"Yes. Filomena Santacroce. Yes."

"You remember that day?"

"I was questioned closely by the police and that Polish reporter."

"Synakowski?"

"Yes. Of course, they questioned me endlessly about this pallbearer. Endlessly and repetitively. The pallbearers brought the casket before the altar and placed it upon the catafalque.

I told them this. Six pallbearers. Three on each side. Then the pallbearers turned and went to the back pews. I told them this. Did I notice anything specific about the pallbearers? One in particular? I told them no, but didn't tell them why, because it was none of their business, but now, in the spirit of openness, which I hope you'll soon join me in, I'll tell you why I didn't pay attention to the pallbearers. If there were twenty-five pallbearers I would not have noticed, my — uh, Eliot."

"It's okay, Father. I call you Father, it's only fair you call me son."

"I am not your father, let's throw away these cold protocols. Your father is Silvio, but if I had a son like you I'd be proud. As Silvio is proud. I'll tell you now where my focus was on that day of murder. After my first year as a priest in Watertown, I entered a Trappist monastery in South Carolina because as a heterosexual who likes — loves to look at women — I wanted a barrier against temptation, because I wanted to keep my vow of chastity, but in the monastery I noticed that some of the brothers did not resist because they could, and did, find consolation in one another. You take my meaning? This only brought to mind what I had given up, and I found the situation terrifically unfair and painful. So I left. I came to Saint Anthony seventeen years ago to live face to face with my heterosexual passion. You know, if a woman smiles at me, Eliot, it is as good as if she — on that day, I was focused on a young woman who sat in the front row. She was beautiful. Her skirt was up over her knees. Her legs were open enough for me to — instead of a whiteness of panties up in there, I saw a patch of darkness, and the soul of Filomena

Santacroce at that moment was in the hands of the Devil.
The pallbearers? Give me a break. I beg you, Eliot, pray for
the repose of my – "

"Eternal soul, Father?"

"My penis."

"Bless me father, for you have sinned."

"Yes, my son, frequently."

To Father G's dismay, Conte gets back on track, "So you
didn't – ?"

"One thing only. One of the pallbearers, I could not say
then or now which, walked in a somewhat odd manner. Perhaps he was drunk. I mentioned this, but neither the police
nor the Polish reporter found that observation to be of any
interest. One of the cops said, 'Some of these old pallbearers
already have one foot in the grave.' He thought he was funny."

"Thank you, Father."

"For what?"

"For sharing your memory."

"I fucked her."

"What?! Who?"

"The woman in the front row. I fucked her every which
way to Sunday, as I believe the saying goes, for a month, and
she was the best p – before I got a hold of myself. That is to
say, when I returned to the not inconsiderable pleasures of
self-abuse."

"You're a witty man, Father."

"Eliot, if you wish to open up, in all seriousness, you
know where I can be found. All will be held in confidence."

Father Gustavo leaves, having not touched his orange
juice. Eliot imagines a fifth of Stolichnaya. Imagines spiking

the O.J. with what it amuses him to think of as "meaning."

––––––––––––––

Conte calls Rudy Synakowski at the *Observer-Dispatch* and
invites him to lunch. Synakowski says, "Thanks, when?"
Conte replies, "Today, at 12:30." Synakowski is startled, but
doesn't show it because he's a supremely composed man, always has been. At Proctor High, he and Conte were distantly
friendly. Distant friendship was a Synakowski specialty. Since
his return to Utica, Conte has seen him at great intervals
for a drink at The Chesterfield. They've never shared a meal.
Synakowski asks, "The Chesterfield?" Conte replies, "My
place. Would pasta *al pesto* be okay?" Synakowski's composure
is almost cracked. Known at Proctor as the Polish Prince, he
resembled the original Polish Prince, the pop singer Bobby
Vinton, though with a cooler, more sharp-edged visage. The
girls he dated had invariably referred to him, with a Mona
Lisa smile, as "Blue Velvet."

After lunch and the polite, meaningless words – Synakowski still nursing his glass of pinot noir, Conte on his third
glass of seltzer – the Polish Prince says, "You have something
on your mind, Detective." It pleases him to address Conte as
"Detective."

"I do, Rudy. A matter of ancient history."

"Shoot."

"Exactly. About a shooting."

"Only one worth talking about, Detective."

"Shall we talk, Rudy?"

"Someone hire you to break the unbreakable case?"

"No."

"Pure, unmercenary curiosity?"

"Yes."

"Sounds ominous."

"You were at Saint Anthony and also wrote the piece on the accident at the Parkway and Oneida Street. I read your articles yesterday."

"You found them fascinating? I take pride in my prose style."

"As well you should. I take it you saw the pallbearer substitution?"

"I didn't – interviews with some onlookers later that day gave me the story and the description. What I was focused on at the time was what everyone wanted to see – the arrival of Aristarco and the Barbones. The level of their security was impressive. Their own goons, of course, and a tight circle of Utica's finest. There was quite a crowd milling around."

"You never saw the pallbearers?"

"I saw them carry the casket into the church. I must have, but have no recall, because… Eliot, why would I? Why would anyone? Nothing remarkable to stick in the mind. It was a funeral fifteen years ago. You have pallbearers at a funeral."

"But you named Raymond DePellaccio in your article."

"Filomena Santacroce's grandniece gave me the name. Later."

"Did you talk to DePellaccio about his convenient lower-back spasm?"

"That's what it seemed like. Convenient. Raymond is the key to the set up. So of course I – not to mention detectives from the force – was eager to talk to him. He was laid up in Saint Elizabeth's for three weeks in traction – under heavy sedation."

"The back thing wasn't – "

"Bullshit? No."

"How do you know he wasn't faking it all the way through? The plan included hospitalization. Why not?"

"I thought of that, Detective. His doctor was Ronald Sheehan. Ring any bells?"

"I've heard the name, but not for some time."

"You've heard the name because he was the most esteemed physician in the area. Honorary degrees, Syracuse and Cornell. You haven't heard his name for some time because he was killed in a one-car accident four months after the assassinations. Your father, who was his patient, delivered the eulogy at Saint Louis Gonzaga, the church where all the faithful Lebanese attend."

"Eventually you must have talked to DePellaccio."

"I intended to, naturally, but I was too late."

"I did a search on him – natural causes according to the obit. When would that have been? Not long after the hospitalization?"

"A week later. Heart attack is how the family wanted it reported. It was suicide. By hanging. In his attic. According to my source in the coroner's office."

"These deaths… this isn't a paranoid movie conspiracy."

"I entertained the thought. Occasionally still do. Where's the evidence, Detective? Good luck."

"You were not at the scene of the van accident, obviously."

"No. There were three witnesses, whom I interviewed."

"You interviewed the driver of the bus and the police-man driving the van?"

"Those were not witnesses, Detective, but I did interview Frank Doolin, you remember Frank? Former mayor, friend of your father's, the bus driver. How the mighty fall. Frank said he had the green light, so did some of his riders, who came forward to see me down at the paper."

"And the van driver? You talked to him?"

"No. Chief Criggy put a clamp on it. Told me when I requested that these good men didn't deserve such publicity. He wouldn't release the names."

"I can't believe a reporter of your, uh…"

"Astuteness?"

Conte toasts the Polish Prince.

"You dug into it, Rudy, I know you did, and determined the name of the driver of the van, didn't you?"

"I didn't have to dig, Eliot – someone came to see me, at home, no less, that night, and told me who it was."

The Polish Prince sips his wine, enjoying the feeling that he has Conte on the edge of his seat.

Conte says, "But that name never appeared in print, ei-ther, as far as I know."

"He spoke on condition that his anonymity would be preserved. Said he feared for his job and his life."

"Would you like to tell me, Rudy?"

"Absolutely, Detective. It gives me pleasure to know that you're looking into the source of the stench. The man who came to see me is our current assistant chief of police, Mi-chael Coca. The man who was driving the van is our current chief – your pal, Antonio Robinson. At the time, I believe they were both corporals. Buddies. Ambitious and on the rise."

Conte breathes out heavily. "You see something dirty, Rudy?"

"Do you? I think you do."

"Some petty jealousy might be all it is, Rudy. Maybe they were rivals of some sort."

"No idea, Detective. What Coca told me was that the light was red – that the van stopped at the light and when the bus hit the intersection the van lurched hard forward – perfectly timed to crash the bus broadside."

"Robinson was maybe spaced out and didn't – " Conte cuts himself off, feigns a shrug. "Maybe Coca lied about the red light."

"Maybe. Maybe. I'm not a grassy-knoll type, except the three witnesses I mentioned had no doubts about the van and the red light and there were no discrepancies among their accounts."

"Their names never appeared in your story. Edited out?"

"Yep."

"Your editor's rationale?"

"He wouldn't give me one."

("Grassy knoll" – not an allusion lost on Conte, who'd written an essay at UCLA on novels about the JFK assassination and its major, explanatory conspiracy theory. When asked by his professor if he, himself, believed that a second shooter, in addition to Oswald, who fired from behind, had fired from a grassy knoll *toward* which Kennedy's limo was heading, Conte replied, I half-believe. To the professor's argument that, psychologically, there was no such thing as half-belief, Conte said, I agree. Nevertheless, I half-believe.)

"From the perspective of the grassy knoll, Rudy, these witnesses were lucky not to be identified, or they would have joined Dr. Sheehan and DePellaccio."

"Your tone is ironic, Detective, but I believe that you believe there was a conspiracy. Who is the spider at the center?"

"Do you by any chance?"

"Have the notes? I certainly do. I'll call the names in to you this afternoon."

"On my land line. You have the number?"

The Polish Prince smiles, says, "I'm a reporter."

"Thanks, Rudy. One more thing. The paper's chief photographer at the time, Enzo Raspante – he's been retired for some time. Is he mentally in order?"

"He's these days at Our Hearts Are Full Assisted Living, up near the college. Has a brother, that's it, who I hear moved to Florida. I'm sure he'd love the company. I visit Enzo occasionally – sharp as a tack and bored."

"Thanks, Rudy."

"One favor, Detective. Should you get to the bottom of the sewer, give me a heads-up."

"I promise."

"We'll do the book and film script together."

Synakowski quaffs the remainder of his wine. Gets up to leave. Conte says, "Wait." Brings him from the freezer a container of frozen pesto sauce. Synakowski thanks him, then adds, "But what will Lisa and I have for dessert, Detective?"

Conte quickly replies, "You could stop by Ricky's – or you could treat your special angel to some special Blue Velvet."

After Synakowski leaves, Conte empties the half-full bottle of wine into the sink. This time with no desire to lean over and inhale.

An hour later, as he's about to leave for Our Hearts Are Full, the phone. Synakowski with the names of the three witnesses to the accident – one dead, the second moved away, address unknown, the third, Nelson Thomas, 414 Ontario Street, no phone. "And one other thing, Detective. Several at the cemetery saw the shooter fall twice as he fled on foot. For what it's worth. They said he seemed clumsy on his feet."

CHAPTER 13

Conte asks the coiffed senior-citizen receptionist at Our
Hearts Are Full if Enzo Raspante is available for visitation.
She responds, "Shall I assume you're a friend or relative?"

"We have a mutual friend at the *Observer-Dispatch*."

"How nice! It's a darn cold day you-know-where when
he gets company. I'll call… Enzo, dear, you have a visitor… A
Mr. Eliot Conte… No, not Connolly… No, not Connery…
CON-TEE… C-O-N-T-E… Just a moment, I'll ask him…
He wants to know if you're Irish… No… he's not, dear…
Enzo… Enzo… I'm Irish and you like me, don't you? That's
very naughty of you to talk that way, Enzo… You know I
won't… He wants to know if you're related to Silvio… Yes, he
is… He's on his way, dear."

Enzo Raspante's living room features a treadmill, dumb-
bells of various weights, photos signed "To Enzo" by Rocky
Marciano and Joe DiMaggio, as well as the usual family pictures. In sweat clothes, Raspante: steel-grey crew cut, little
hair loss, none of the obvious collapses about the face and
neck, a flat stomach. At eighty-three, he looks like an extremely fit sixty-year-old who could pass for mid-fifties.

He shakes Conte's hand, "You got me in the middle of

my daily workout," and proceeds to do fifteen rapid push-ups and twenty-five squats. Offers Conte a seat, "So what the heck is a man of my tip-top condition doing in this place? Walkers and wheelchairs galore, they constantly stare into space, odors of an unmistakable, drooling at the dinner table? Not to mention late-afternoon concerts given by off-key twelve-year-olds? My choice was to live alone without family, and friends all dead or with Alzheimer's, what's the difference, and who comes over except Rudy Synakowski once in a while, I'm glad to meet you, Mr. Conte. I chose, as you can see, without hesitation, the droolers and the incontinent. I'm a little hard of hearing. I have a car and can come and go as I please, but I rarely go. Shall we go off-campus or is this acceptable?"

Conte tells him what he does for a living and that he's come to see him about photos he may have taken on a legendary day, fifteen years ago at Saint Anthony, when Filomena Santacroce's coffin was carried into the church.

"Silvio's son's a private eye? Why didn't I know that? I knew and forgot it on the road to dementia? You're in luck, Eliot. I kept negatives of tens of thousands over a fifty-year period, but when I made the move here, I dumped everything except a box of special things – mostly my kids when they were little, got married, you know... they live now in Miami, Santa Fe, Chicago... Larry, my oldest... Larry. Yes. I see them once a year, if I'm lucky. The grandchildren... yes... tell the truth – am I too garrulous? Excessive garrulity is a sign. There are a few folders relating to very special events of a public nature, like the one you're interested in. That was a big doozy. Everything nicely labeled."

"Enzo, the shot of the mobsters arriving at the church that appeared in the paper and was picked up by the major – "

"That's the one he wanted – the boss looked at the others but decided on that one."

"You had shots of the pallbearer exchange?"

"Does the bear do number two in the woods?"

Raspante excuses himself, goes to the bedroom closet, returns with a folder. "Here we are." They move to the couch, go through the file, isolate five negatives of interest.

"Who said no, Enzo, to the pallbearer shots?"

"Editor-in-chief. Rudy and I at the time discussed this *pezzo di merda*. We have our theories. Rudy calls them the grassy knoll perspective."

"Who was editor-in-chief at the time?"

"Still is. Sanford T. Whitaker. That high-toned WASP who's been writing editorials against your father for years. Thinks his shit doesn't stink. Your father the corrupt political boss, this and that. Tell you what, I'll get these developed by tomorrow afternoon. Ordinarily, it'd take a week, but Donny at Daniels' Photography is a friend of mine."

"Didn't you show these photos to the police?"

"To Chief Criggy himself, who must've buried them, because nothing was ever done that I know of."

"But you had the freedom to contact other news outlets and sell your photos for a bundle, I'd guess, and that way it would have been nationally publicized in a hurry – the image of the shooter, no? The *National Inquirer*? The *New York Post*?"

"Did I say they were my pictures?"

"Who else's would they be?"

"Up to four days, Detective, before Filomena Santacroce was buried in Calvary Cemetery, everything I shot was technically mine. But I never had a contract. Nobody below Sanford had a contract. We got paid twice a month, that was it. I was no big-deal photographer working for the *New York Times* on a cushy contract. You follow me? Then four days before she's buried, Sanford calls me in and offers me a five-year contract with a twenty-percent raise. Because my work is so wonderful, he says, for so many years, and it's about time the paper showed its gratitude. So I signed right on the spot! What the fuck did I need to read the contract for, which when I read it, one hour after he says the pallbearer shots are not going in, I find out that what I signed says I own nothing. The paper owns my photos from now on, and if I violate the contract I lose my job and get sued on top of it, and where can I at that age get another job in this area that's equivalent? Now you have them, you're the right man, and I hope to Christ you'll raise holy hell."

"Would you like to have dinner at my house tomorrow night? I'm a decent cook."

"Being of sound mind and wishing to stay of sound body, I don't allow myself to drive at night."

"I'll pick you up at 5:30. How's that?"

"I'll be good to go, Houston."

Conte rises to leave.

"Enzo, I can't thank you enough."

"Tell me something, Detective, do you sense a comic quality to my personality?"

"You're a delight, Enzo."

"Tell me something else. Do you think people on the

dementia superhighway are as effortlessly humorous as I am?"

"Never, Enzo."

"Would you join me now in a cup of coffee, Detective, so that we might enjoy everyday chatter? The Yankees and so forth? It would please me greatly if you would. Please, linger awhile."

"I'll take mine black with sugar."

"Detective Conte, I am not the man I used to be. That's my truth. What's yours?"

"I was never the man I used to be."

CHAPTER 14

Home from Our Hearts Are Full, Conte finds a UPS package at the front door: his new BlackBerry. At his desk: the light flashes on the answering machine. Tom Castellano:

> Eliot, the mystery of Mrs. Kinter and child is solved. I got a FedEx letter this afternoon from Reading, Pennsylvania. Here's what it says: "I want to thank you so much for being such a nice landlord and I am so sorry for leaving without saying good-bye. I am not coming back ever and please do not disclose my location to my so-called husband under no circumstances please." Hope that relieves your mind, El. To be honest, I think you have the type mind that can't be relieved because they haven't yet invented that type laxative. Come on over and see me sometime, big boy.

Opens e-mail. One new message: Robinson:

> What's going on with the thing? Why is it so tough to see you since Sunday morning? The thing needs

elimination one way or the other. The longer we wait, the worse.

Conte replies:

> Have devised the strategy. Millicent tells me she and Denise are still very close. Need M to take D out of town for the weekend. Suggest NYC for Broadway shows. Get her out of town Friday thru Sunday and all will be well. Out of touch until the thing is cured. Trust me.

E-mails Synakowski:

> Rudy, what can you tell me about your colleague Jed Kinter?

Goes to the bathroom, flosses and brushes teeth. Changes shirt. Returns to his desk. Synakowski has answered:

> Not much. No friends here that I know of. Competent in what he does. Walks by without saying hello or returning a greeting. A stranger to basic civilities. A short man. One thing: it was Whitaker who brought him in fifteen years ago. He visits Sanford's office once a week and Sanford draws the blinds. Enzo used to say it's all about fellatio. When I asked Enzo if he thought Kinter was brought in to give Sanford head, Enzo said he was convinced it was the other way around. A leading theory at the paper

is that Sanford plays in the closet. Here's something else that will whet your appetite. Enzo once got into the personnel files, don't know how, a long time back. We all have them – background experience etc. No file on Kinter. Find the spider at the center.

Notebook in hand he heads off to dine at The Chesterfield, the most Italian of restaurants in Italian Utica, on Bleecker, a ten-minute walk from home and about 100 yards from Nelson Thomas' residence, around the corner, at 414 Ontario. Conte dines at The Chesterfield twice a week, where they know and care for him well.

Two entrances. One to the bar, the other to the dining room – a long rectangular space with a short wall of windows giving onto Bleecker, and at the opposite end, swinging doors to the kitchen. One of the long walls paneled in darkly stained knotty pine, with signed photos of Jerry Vale, Vic Damone, and Perry Como. Opposite this wall of heroes, a wall of artistically ruined brick. Tables covered in red-and-white checkered cloth. Conte sits at the table closest to the kitchen. Two couples at the other end.

He assumes he's entered the dining area unseen, but less than a minute after sitting down, Rosie Pontenero, the owner's wife, appears with a Johnnie Walker on the rocks, saying, "You're not getting enough sleep. Too much on your mind, El?"

"What's on my mind, Rosie, are three hot peppers stuffed with sausage, a bowl of the greens, and a large Coke."

"Anything else?"

"Some extra garlic bread."

"That it, sweetheart?"

"Not hungry tonight, Rosie."

As soon as she disappears into the kitchen, Conte takes his drink quickly to the rest room and pours it into the toilet. He's back at the table just before she returns with the garlic bread and Coke.

"Another Johnnie, El?"

"I'm good."

"I always thought so," stroking his shoulder. "We love you here. Keep it in mind, sad eyes."

"I love you too, Rosie."

"Dom and I are trying to think of a perfect lady for you, on the thought I'm not available. Sit tight, dear, I'll give you the salad."

He has no strategy for "the thing." Has no idea why he'd committed to resolving "the thing" by the weekend. E-mails Robinson from his BlackBerry and asks if Michael C has a favorite drink that he indulges in after work. Rosie brings the chicory and dandelion greens in olive oil and lemon juice – known at The Chesterfield as Utica Greens. Halfway through the greens, Robinson responds:

Campari on the rocks, nightly, since I've known him.
We had dinner at each other's all the time. Always
Campari on the rocks.

Conte asks if C has a security system. Answer:

Too fucking cheap.

Conte:

> Let me know if M has arranged NYC as soon as
> possible.

He's setting a detailed process in place, of specific actions,
but to what end? Get in the house. Slip it into the Campari.
Come back that night to find Coca in a deep, drug-induced
sleep, helpless, unable to lift a finger. On the living room
floor, at his mercy. Then what? Strip him naked, tie him up,
wrist to ankles. To what end? Then what? Turn out all the
lights. Wake him with high-concentrate smelling salts. Dis-
guise himself. Including the voice. Think of a costume. Then
what? To what end? Buy two dildos. Then? Turn on the lights.
Conte opens his notebook and sketches a spiderweb with the
name "Sanford T. Whitaker" at the center. Sketches another
web with the name "Eliot Conte" at the center and two
moths caught in the web, drained of life, and labeled "Rosalind" and "Emily."

"El, dear!" Rosie with the stuffed peppers and a refill of
the Coke. He looks up. "Come back from wherever the heck
you are and come with me to the kitchen. You need first aid!
My God, El! Look at what you've done to those cuticles!
Let's not worry about the tablecloth, sweetie. Lord! Look at
what you've done to yourself!"

After Rosie takes care of his hands – after he's eaten
everything on his plate and all the garlic bread – after he's
paid the tab – he's out on the street, the night turned upstate
late-October cold, shivering in his sports jacket, turning the
corner on Ontario as a man leaves 414 in jogging gear. A

stocky African-American, *Hut! HutHut!* Down Ontario he goes, away from Conte, down Gilbert he goes, gone.

Collar turned up against the wind and shoulders hunched against the cold, Conte tracks The Runner down Gilbert, where at its foot Conte turns left along Broad. (Should he have turned right? Where is Nelson Thomas?) On this ill-lit east-west thoroughfare he walks brooding through the devastated old industrial district – roughhouse saloons, broken beer bottles, drifting fast-food trash and the occasional condom, sagging with semen, from chain-link fences hung with care. And there they are – the haunted block-long buildings, those hulking brick corpses where once his mother and her friends worked in the textile mills. Reinhabited in the 1960s by General Electric, now long vacated for good. At the corner of Gilbert and Broad, where he began his brooding journey, what he never noticed. In deep weeds, alongside a baby carriage without wheels, an actual corpse.

CHAPTER 15

Conte can't shake the chill, even after turning up the heat and donning his newly (online) acquired Icelandic sweater. At his desk, googles "mickey": named for an infamous Chicago bartender. Among options: chloral hydrate: red with a slightly bitter taste. Perfect: like Campari. Problem: prescription only. Could ask boyhood-pal-become-pharmacist, but won't put Vince on the spot. Rintrona wants to help. About to call him when he hears footsteps on the front porch and the door swings open and Antonio Robinson walks in with Eliot's hard cover copy of *Moby-Dick*, which he tosses from three feet away, thunderous onto the desk.

"Couldn't put the son of a bitch down, El. I'm the ship, man, but I'm not going down. *This* Pequod," tapping his chest, "me, I don't go down."

Robinson paces.

"But that's not how Melville's story ends, Robby."

"But that's how our story ends. We survive, we two alone. The motherfuckin' white whale doesn't."

"Michael C doesn't survive?"

"Loosely speaking."

"Best book ever written, some say, anywhere, any time."

"Oh yeah? That a fact, Professor? I took two lit courses at Syracuse. Lit for Jocks. Know what I say about literature, all due respect, El? Fuck literature, what I say. Because it's worthless when you really need to get something *done*."

"Somehow I don't think you're here to discuss the practical value of Melville's masterpiece."

"I'm here to discuss and assess *your* practical value. You tell me you have devised a strategy. I like that word. Stra-te-gy. The word of a practical man. Now I need detail."

"Don't trust me, Robby?"

"I fear you're impotent to act because you're distracted with this fuckin' Kinter. I think you're not devoting yourself to the real thing. I think you're grieving for your kids, no matter what you say."

"Don't tell me what I'm doing with my time."

Robinson pulls up a chair. "Let's have a drink and relax a while, shall we?"

Conte brings him a Johnnie Walker on the rocks, seltzer for himself. Robinson nods in approval:

"You're going ascetic? This is good. Denying yourself? This is very good. You chose the path of the philosophical assassin? In Lit for Jocks, we read a comic book version of *Crime and Punishment*. You'll work toward total clarity. You'll burn off all purposes except one. You'll be on edge for the thing. You'll drive the edge right through his fat fuckin' throat. According to the comic book version. El, I'm impressed with the dedication." He toasts Conte and says, "You're on the path to what you've needed to do for a very long time."

"You want Michael dead, don't you?"

"This is how I see it, El. There's the mild-mannered

professor type. Soft-spoken. A harmless bear of a man. My sweet friend for life. An obsessive reader of serious writing, a connoisseur of Italian opera, but Italian opera is the bridge to another man – the man of extremity and crazy ass passions. This other man is the man who made a dangerous UCLA exit. He's the man of violence on the train. The rage monster within. Dr. Conte and Mr. Eliot."

"You want Michael dead, don't you?"

"His fate is in your hands. Whatever you do, I know he'll never again bother – "

"*You?*"

"*Women.* Me? Yes. Me as Chief of Police with the sacred responsibility to keep Utica safe for the innocent. What are you, all of a sudden? Casting aspersions? My dear wife had a feeling. She had an inkling due to your line of questioning. Millicent believes you're not to be trusted to do the right thing."

"What do you believe, Robby?"

"I think you're my only friend. I think in every way we're brothers. I think we share a father, though you'd never put it that way. He loves us both equally. Yes, he does, El, don't contradict me. Don't you dare contradict. I think you want to help me. I know you want to help. I need you, El."

"I will help you. When I get through with Michael C he'll never…"

"What? Finish the thought. Give me detail. What about the Campari?"

"I'll tell you nothing. Because you need deniability."

"El, I can't tell you how much – "

"Shut up."

Robinson is suddenly afraid.

"Why did you lie to me, Robby?"

"Lie?"

"You deaf?"

"About what?"

"The rapes. You lied."

"You'll help anyway? Even though you think I lied, which I definitely did not."

"I'll help anyway."

"El, are you going to hurt me?"

"Shut up and listen. You lied. Come clean now."

Looking at the floor, Antonio says, "El."

"I'll take that as an admission that you lied."

"It won't keep you from helping?"

"No. And don't ever ask me that question again."

"When? When will you neutralize him?"

"I intend to wrap everything up by this weekend. Now you can help by telling me about the so-called accident you had fifteen years ago on the Parkway at Oneida. On the way to the cemetery. You were the driver, but it was kept out of the press and you never told me about it when I returned from Austria. Why not?"

"I was embarrassed to tell you. A humiliation, like fumbling in the end zone. I had blood on my hands. How did you find out?"

"Michael was on that van."

"You know that too?"

"He's blackmailing you? Is that it?"

"Yes."

"About what?"

"He's saying I did it deliberately."

"And he waits fifteen years to put the screws to you, Robby? Makes no sense."

"Tell me about it."

"Don't lie to me."

"I lied about the rapes, I did, but about this – I'm where you are. Makes no sense to me either why he'd wait fifteen years. I need another drink, El."

"What does he want from you?"

"To step down as chief so that he can be elevated."

Conte pours him a double.

"No ice, El?"

"Ran out."

"I know you got ice. Trying to get me drunk so I'll spill all the beans?"

"Yes."

"No more beans to spill, bro."

"Did you deliberately jump the light?"

"No."

"Frank Doolin, riders on the bus, witnesses on the street, and Michael all say you jumped the light. Michael says deliberately."

"How do you know Michael claims deliberately? You talk to him?"

"No."

"How do you know?"

"My business how I know."

"I don't dispute I could've jumped the light. But deliberate? No way. Because why would I?"

"What is Michael saying about why?"

"Nothing."

"He's saying to you that you didn't want to get to the cemetery. That you were in on the triple assassination. You and DePellaccio were the links to success. Michael has some kind of proof, doesn't he?"

"I agree about DePellaccio. It's obvious."

"You're fuckin with me, Robby."

"Trust me, El."

"After you tell me this: Why did you and Millicent concoct this ridiculous rape story when all you had to do is tell your beloved brother the truth about Michael's blackmail?"

"Because if I did, I knew you'd think what Michael C thinks. That I was in on it."

"And why would I come to that conclusion?"

"I don't know. I just think you might've."

"Because it's true? Because you're dirty? Because deep down you want me to know? Because you're guilty?"

"Why would I want you to know? Assuming it's true? You're losing me, Prof. I can't keep up with your prof mind, Prof."

"The ultimate test of loyalty. What kids say when they're little. Daddy, if I commit a bad crime, will you protect me from the police? Will you lie for me, Daddy?"

"You said that to Silvio at one time?"

"Shut up."

"You're not my daddy. We're not blood brothers, El."

"But if I shield you and help you while knowing that you were involved in a conspiracy to commit murder, then my loyalty is the same as a blood relation's. Greater even, much greater, because we're not blood related. Because blood relations have been known to tear out and eat each other's intestines. Loyalty in the face of criminal knowledge is the truest proof of the deepest, unbreakable bond – beyond blood. Only the unshakably loyal are family, forget about blood."

"I love what you say, El, but you don't have to face this loyalty test. I wasn't a conspirator in murder. Believe me, please."

"I want to."

"You're eating Silvio's intestines?"

"Drop it."

"And eating your own intestines over the kids you lost. In Lit for Jocks, Professor Terhune taught us about puns. I got an 'A' in the course. That was his big theme. Puns. For example, this Kinter. Who is he? He's your kin. You see yourself as an accomplice to the murder of your daughters. You abused them by leaving them. Kinter is you, El. Kill him and you commit suicide without having to die. Why are you shivering, man, in this hot house?"

Robinson places his hand on Conte's forehead.

"I think you have a fever. Got any of those chicken broth bouillon cubes in the cabinet? Good. I'll make you some hot soup. Aspirin in the bathroom? Good. I'll get you a couple."

Before Robinson leaves, Eliot says, "I'll give you a clue. I'm going to ram the fear of Our Lord et cetera."

Robinson smiles, says, "Dr. Conte, let me introduce you to your truth, Mr. Eliot."

———————————

He makes two calls after Robinson leaves. The first to Rin-trona, who will have the chloral hydrate on Thursday noon at the Q Shack. No problem.

"The smelling salts, Bobby?"

"A cloth dipped in ammonia followed by a pail of cold water will do the job."

"Bobby, I'll need your help in Utica on Friday night. I can't do this alone."

"Do what, Eliot?"

"I'll explain when we meet why I need a partner."

"You got one, Eliot."

"Not a word of this to Catherine, Bobby."

"Not a word, Eliot."

"One other thing, Bobby."

"What's that?"

"Buy one of those tight rubber clown masks that covers the skull and gives you a bald head with a few red tufts over the ears. Preferably a happy-face clown."

The second call is to Catherine Cruz. Dinner Thursday night?

"Yes," she says, "where?"

"I'm driving down."

"I'll cook," she says.

Tomorrow, no later than 10:00 A.M. Pacific Coast time, Nancy Norwald will receive his FedEx package.

CHAPTER 16

It's 7:30 Wednesday morning and Conte awakes aching with a fever of 101.5° and a plan for the day. He manages a cup of coffee, black, and one egg white. About to leave when he decides to avoid fever-induced dehydration by forcing down two twelve-ounce glasses of water. (He'll regret this.) Then, bundled up for the 32° morning, drives down to 414 Ontario Street and knocks on the front door of Nelson Thomas, the African-American runner and only available witness, according to Synakowski, to the disputed accident fifteen years back. No response. Knocks again as he recalls information from the most recent city directory: Nelson Thomas is the sole occupant of 414 Ontario, a two-family house. Glances at front window. A sign affixed: KISS ME I'M ITALIAN. Extended knocking. No response. Conte needs to pee.

Exhausted, he goes home, relieves himself (weakly: enlarged prostate), then back to bed and sleeps until 11:00. Upon waking, picks his BlackBerry off the bedside table and e-mails Rudy Synakowski:

Need a favor which I can't ask of Robinson. Can you get me the promotion history with dates of the

Chief and Coca? From the time they entered training? ASAP. Thanks. – E.

Synakowski responds immediately:

Working against deadline. Give me a couple of hours and you'll have it. – R.
P.S. Memo from the grassy knoll. This just in: Nelson Thomas of 414 Ontario Street found dead last night in the street around 8:30 on Gilbert near Broad. Victim of an apparent hit and run driver. Autopsy pending.

(*"Whack job." "I think he wants to communicate with me." "Why you? About what?"*)

From the refrigerator he takes the seven remaining bottles of the Czech import and empties them into the sink. His house is now an alcohol-free zone. Digging again into his cuticles. Feels nothing. An emptiness within, signifying nothing.

In the car again, Conte eats a chocolate bar for energy, drives to the Hannaford Supermarket where he (not yet free of alcohol desire) takes from the cooler a six-bottle carton of the nonalcoholic beer Excaliber, then heads on to Oneida First National Bank to pay his weekly visit to Donatella ("Tootsie") Tomasi, bank manager and his godmother Angie's daughter. In the parking lot, Conte chugs down one of the Excalibers, thinks about doing another, but doesn't – through the doors of Oneida First National directly he goes to the Men's Room.

Donatella Tomasi looks up as he enters her office, "Jeez! You don't look well! What's wrong, El?"

"Maybe coming down with a little something, Tootsie. No big deal."

"Maybe?!"

Tootsie Tomasi is a dark-haired and full-bodied beauty, fifty years old and always unlucky in love – because ever since Eliot returned twenty years ago she had nurtured a crush on him so hidden, even from herself, that she barely knew she had one, which is why the many suitors who were attracted never felt she was wholly *there*, especially in the most intimate moments. Oh, she knows, alright, but prefers not to. Daily life is a little easier that way. Conte's weekly visits and occasional lunch dates make her happy – and unhappy. Conte knows – he's known for years.

They sit on the small couch. Conte tells her that his visit is regrettably, this time, not social and that he thinks she might be able to assist him in an important investigation. She replies that she's happy to help "unless, well, are you talking to me now in my official capacity here with access to sensitive information? In which case, El, you know, as much as I'd – I'm sure you understand, I'm sorry, only the police can get that from us."

"I don't mean to make you uncomfortable, Toots."

"Uncomfortable? You? Listen, no harm can come from telling me the story. We're talking. It's just talk."

"It concerns a famous Utica event. Fifteen years ago."

"Don't tell me!"

"That's what I'm telling you."

"Don't tell me you have a lead!"

"I'm telling you that."

She gets up. Calls her secretary and asks him to hold all calls and clients. Closes the door.

"Strictest confidence, Toots. If my godmother were still with us, I'd say, Okay, tell her, but no one else. Can't tell you how much I miss Angie. She stepped in when my mother died and never stepped away."

"Remember those calzones, El! She hated cooking, unless it was for you and me."

He takes her hand. He knows what he's doing, though he'd rather not know.

"Just between us, Toots."

"I promise."

"Raymond DePellaccio."

"Who's he?"

"Died not long after those murders."

"Okay."

"Hypothetically, Toots. Let's say a bank official from another bank calls about an account you might be carrying. Do you tend to honor that?"

"That's a gray area, El."

"In other words?"

"An extremely gray area."

"So if DePellaccio were not one of yours?"

"Was he the killer?"

"No. He was part of a conspiracy along with someone else you definitely have heard of."

"Who?"

He lets go of her hand. "Can't say at this time."

"Okay."

Takes her hand again.

"Hypothetically, Toots, if a customer brings in a large amount of cold cash for deposit, what do you do?"

"We take it."

"Just like that?"

"Just like that. Naturally, we run a counterfeit test. We take it, El, because that's what we are."

"What you *do*, Toots?"

"I didn't misspeak, Professor. What we are. Moneytakers."

He excuses himself and goes to the men's room. When he returns, she's working at her computer. He sits on the couch. She stays at her desk. She thinks he's deteriorating by the minute. She goes to the couch and takes his hand:

"I've been wanting to call you all week, El. I won't beat around the bush. You were married a long time ago out there in California to a Nancy, who divorced you and then quickly remarried a Nor something, right? And changed your kids' names to Nor something with your consent. Your father mentioned this to me and Angie many years ago while the three of us were playing pinochle at our house. Silvio couldn't understand why you let her change their names. When he told us, he cried. El, I saw that terrible story on CNN concerning Nancy Norwald, who they think murdered her children. I'm worried that's the reason you look sick. Was that your ex, God forbid?"

"No need to worry, Toots. The Nancy I married – she married a guy named Norwalk."

"Thank God her name isn't Norwald."

"Thank God, Toots."

"You say thank God, but you don't believe, do you? Tell the truth, El."

"I don't know."

"You want coffee or something?"

"No thanks."

"You don't know if you believe or not? That's one I haven't heard before. Your father believes."

"In what?"

"God. Who else? You know, he calls me here every Friday afternoon without fail."

"How nice of him."

"Gosh, El, you should cut him some slack. He's very sweet. Always tells me I'm the daughter he never had. I say Eliot is the son Angie never had. At the end of every call it's always about you. Because he knows I see you once a week and figures if he calls on Friday, you know what I'm saying. How's my son, Toots? You see him more than I do. Maybe I should take a job in the bank as your assistant. Joking around like that but I know – "

"Toots, how many times have we been over this?"

"A lot, El. I feel sorry for him. And you. The three of us have so much in common."

"That's one I haven't heard before."

"It's obvious, Professor. Silvio lived his whole life in Utica. Like me. And except for going off to California for college – you came back here, El, didn't you? Because this is where we take you in when you're in a situation. You made the decision to return when you were in trouble out there. The old neighborhood – where you were raised – where you're known and you know you are known. If you only stayed put you wouldn't have had the heartbreak. I know, I know – Utica is no bed of roses, but it's your place. You came back to stay, but you never wrapped your arms around your decision. Am I offending you, El, because if I am – "

"You're right about everything, Toots. Anyway, thanks for the chat. I think I'll go home and rest. Maybe lunch next week?"

"After that pain-in-the-you-know-where speech I made, you still want to go to lunch?"

"Of course. We're family. Like brother and sister." His response wounds her to the core.

He goes to the door.

"Wait. It helps for congestion." She gives him two tablets of a decongestant, which she's wrapped in tissue.

"Stay in touch, Toots."

Before exiting the bank, another trip to the men's room, to stand at the urinal, staring down hunched over the pathetic stream. Tosses decongestants in the waste basket. In the car, a swig of Excaliber. Decongestants, he knows, are not indicated for men with enlarged prostates. Eliot Conte, he knows, is not indicated for Tootsie Tomasi.

At home, two aspirin and a double dosage of a medication which eases the urine for men with his problem, and then to bed.

At the bank, Donatella Tomasi calls Silvio Conte and tells him that his son is coming down with something and that he made up a story, he lied about "that woman in California... No, he didn't make up any stories about you... I swear to God... (She laughs.) No, he didn't suggest you were behind

September 11th... or the Kennedy assassination... Can I bring you anything from Ricky?... (She laughs.) I'll ask but I don't believe Ricky sells filial devotion... I agree, I do, Daddy, that after a certain age we have nothing left to rely on but our sense of humor... Not true... I'm getting to that age."

Conte awakes at 2:00 P.M. Has Synakowski responded?

> Hi Eliot, Another memo from the grassy knoll: Robinson and Coca graduate from Central New York Police Academy, Onondaga Community College, Syracuse, June 1990. Patrolmen until 1993. Both promoted to corporal same week 1994. At time of triple murder 1995 still corporals. 5 months later January 1996 both promoted to sergeant same week. 1997 they make lieutenant same week. 2 years later 1999 they're inspectors same week. 3 years later 2002 Robinson elevated to deputy chief but Coca has to wait another year to make deputy chief. 3 years after making deputy Robinson becomes assistant chief 2005. 2 years later 2007 Robinson is made chief and Coca assistant chief. Here's something interesting: the Bobbsey Boys apply to the Academy on the same day. You owe me, Eliot. Pesto for 10 years.

Having seen the error of his ways, his fever unabated, Conte will risk dehydration and resolves to take no more liquids – with the exception of that cup of steaming chicken bouillon and three swigs of Excaliber which comprise the entirety of his late lunch. He calls Enzo Raspante to say that he must renege on his dinner invitation because of flu-like symptoms and Raspante replies, "Me too, who gave it to who? I don't remember a romantic episode, do you?" Conte replies that he doesn't "recall it either, but my memory isn't what it used to be." Raspante tells him that he'll call Donny and "give the okay to give the photos to you whenever." An hour later, Enzo calls to tell him the photos are waiting.

He picks up the photos and, too eager to wait until he gets home to examine them, begins to open one of the smaller envelopes when a late-model BMW pulls up a few parking spaces away. The driver emerges and walks hurriedly into Donny's. The driver is Jed Kinter. Confident that he hasn't been noticed, his paranoia on the rise, Conte drives rapidly away.

He's spreading out five eight-by-tens on his desk. Arraying the larger ones on the floor. The eight-by-tens include DePellaccio (*great fuckin' actor*) in back spasm, face contorted, bent over, at the rear of the hearse, casket not yet withdrawn; a man from behind in a black suit at the rear right side of the casket, hoisting; casket at the foot of the steps to Saint Anthony and the man in the black suit, dark glasses, visible in profile; casket still at the foot of the steps and the man in three-quarters profile glancing at the camera; man in black from behind, casket at open doors of the church. The five photos on the floor are detail eighteen-by-twenty-four blow-ups of the man in black. He appears to match the description given by Janice McPherson.

Conte's fever is down to 99.5°. He's suddenly quite hungry, but has no energy for cooking. Takes a package of Genoa salami from the refrigerator and eats five slices. A handful of spicy olives. Four Ritz crackers slathered with peach jelly. A few modest swigs of Excaliber. Opens his computer and searches the archive of the *Observer-Dispatch*. The day of the murders was a day of heavy overcast with a threat of light showers. (*Dark glasses*.) He calls Janice McPherson at the college. Could she meet for coffee, say, at 8:00?... How about the Wendy's at Oneida Square?... Okay, your house... Some photos I need to show you...Yes, Janice, related to our discussion.

No sooner does he put the phone down than it rings. Tootsie: "El, I can't put this in an e-mail, which is why I'm calling. Raymond DePellaccio deposited nine thousand dollars, in 450 twenty-dollar bills, one week before the murders. He was one of ours. He withdrew all of it about five weeks later. Jeez, I shouldn't be doing this."

EC: I owe you, Toots.

TT: Just between us. I could get fired.

EC: Of course. One more thing, Toots.

TT: *Madon'*! When will this end?

EC: What can you tell me about Antonio Robinson?

TT: I can't do that.

EC: I understand.

TT: This is crazy... I'm searching... One of ours

from way back… Nothing in the period you're interested in.

EC: Thanks, Toots. I'll bother you no more.

TT: Feeling any better?

EC: I'll survive. Call you soon.

TT: Who else can I tell you about?

EC: When we have lunch, tell me all about you.

TT: You're nice, El.

EC: Talk to you later.

TT: Hope so.

EC: Soon, Toots.

———————————

In a light rain, Conte hurries to her door. It opens before he has the chance to knock. She's dressed to kill. He thinks she's attractive. He thinks she's ready for some action. He wants to banish the thought, and does, sort of.

"This weather," she says. "Utica."

"Good evening, Janice."

They sit at the dining room table, which is set with expensive china and silverware. A carrot cake and homemade chocolate chip cookies.

She says, "Coffee? Tea?"

He wants to say neither, already feeling the urge to pee. Instead, he says, "You wouldn't happen to have ginger twist, would you, Janice?"

She replies that she does and adds, with apparent irrelevance, "My son is out of town on business." He understands the relevance.

She goes to the kitchen. He calls out, "Could you tell me where the restroom is?"

"Of course I could!" Laughing, warm and soft.

When he returns, she's pouring his tea, saying "I decided to have what you're having, Detective."

"It's nice tea. Hope you enjoy it."

"I'll enjoy it, Detective, why wouldn't I if you do?"

He's thinking, It's been a while, approximately 114 years. Why not? He says, "I'm eager for you to see these photos."

"What are they of?"

"I really can't be sure, which is where you come in. Tell me what you think. There's no right or wrong."

"Okay."

He's thinking, Too sick to give her what she's after. Maybe what I'm after.

"Detective, if I may say so, tonight you don't look quite like yourself."

"Who do I look like, Janice? George Clooney?"

She smiles and says, "Oh, you know what I mean. Are you feeling okay?"

"A little off, but okay enough. (*But not enough to.*) Showing her now the eight-by-tens.

After a moment she says, "Are you showing me what I think? He looks like... hard to say, really. I think, though... fifteen years is a long time."

"Look at these," showing her the blow-ups.

"That's Jed's visitor!"

"You're positive?"

"Absolutely one-hundred percent! Why is he at a funeral?"

"Why indeed."

"This is mysterious."

"It is and it isn't."

"You won't tell me?"

"After I solve the mystery."

He's sipping his tea, very small sips. Considering the low-cut blouse, unbuttoned down to her – enjoying the carrot cake immensely when she picks up two of the blow-ups, the full-length profile and three-quarter shots, and says, "I'm seeing something I bet you didn't see, Detective."

"What's that?"

"Guess!"

"Please, Janice."

"We women tend to see these things. We're like detectives in our own way. Detectives of fashion."

"Come on, Janice, stop teasing me."

"Look at his shoes!"

"Okay."

"And?"

"The soles. The heels. Is that it?"

"Those are special, Detective. We women can buy these platform shoes in a shoe store, but a man – why, I think you'd need to have them specially made. Not *you*, of course, you're certainly tall and – but one of these shorties with complexes? You know how they are."

"Great cake, Janice." (*They said he seemed clumsy on his feet.*)

"Can't say I made it, but if you allow me the pleasure of your company another time and give me fair warning, I'll homemake you something real special."

"And I'll look forward to it, Janice."

"Shall we get back on track, Detective?"

"That day the visitor left Kinter's apartment, you described it as hot and humid."

"It was during that awful heat wave."

"Hot and humid you said?"

"Yes."

"Sunny or overcast?"

"That's beyond me, I'm afraid. Have I failed you? At the crucial point?"

"Far from it. Anything else strike you?"

She studies the blow-ups. Shakes her head in disappointment. She's crestfallen. He puts his hand on hers. "You did great, Janice. You helped. Another time in a nonprofessional situation, maybe you'll allow me the pleasure of sampling your specialty of the house?"

"No maybe about it, Eliot."

Her refusal to pretend to remember whether the day in question was sunny or overcast convinces him that she's a solid witness. He gets up. An intimate hug, initiated by Janice, enjoyed by both.

On the way home, Conte is struck by a wave of nausea. Stops the car, opens the door, leans out and vomits violently.

———————————

He's in bed at 9:15, about to turn out the light on his bedside table when he decides he must call Enzo Raspante. Picks up his intimate bedside mate:

ER: That thing I thought I was coming down with?

I'm not. You sound like you got it. You sound bad, kid.

EC: Enzo, I need to ask you a question. Do you recall one of your co-workers named Jed Kinter?

ER: Quiet. Not too friendly. That's about it. Kept to himself. That's it.

EC: Any proclivity you might have sensed?

ER: What's that mean? Proclivity?

EC: Put it this way. Did he have a special relationship with Sanford Whitaker?

ER: Nobody has a special relationship with that holier-than-thou son of a bitch.

EC: Put it this way. You never suspected that Whitaker and Kinter were sucking each other off?

ER: You running a fever or smoking something?

EC: You never told a co-worker that Kinter was seeing Whitaker in his office about fellatio?

ER: Detective Conte, I recommend lots of fluids, two aspirin every four to six hours, and as much sleep as you can get. If you don't feel better in a couple of days, see a doctor. Good night, Detective, and pray to the Virgin Mother to be relieved of your affliction.

One more call to make. The automated voice at FedEx responds to his enunciation of the tracking number and tells him that delivery was made at 9:58 A.M. Pacific Coast time and signed by N. Norwald.

CHAPTER 17

After five and a half hours of sleep, uncompromised by his treacherous prostate, Eliot Conte is hyperalert at 3:35 A.M. – fever broken, anxiety rising. Three proven liars: Antonio Robinson, Millicent Robinson, Rudy Synakowski. He understands the motives of the Robinsons, but Synakowski? Why would he invent a sexual connection between Sanford Whitaker and Jed Kinter? And why had Whitaker suppressed the photos of the substitute pallbearer? And why would De-Pellaccio commit suicide after withdrawing the $9,000 he'd deposited just a few weeks before? DePellaccio was murdered. Was he not? By whom? The substitute pallbearer? Was he, Eliot Conte, the last to see Nelson Thomas alive as Thomas jogged down Gilbert to his death? Hit-and-run accident, or hit-and-run murder? But why, after fifteen years, would Nelson Thomas suddenly be targeted? Aside from Synakowski and Whitaker, who knew that Thomas had witnessed the police van crash the bus? Robinson? Who ran down Thomas? Was his, Eliot Conte's, interest in Nelson Thomas, Thomas' death warrant? Fortuitous that Kinter appeared at Donny Daniels' Photography just after Conte collected the photos? Donny alerted him? Donny himself was involved? (*Surely not Enzo Raspante. Surely not.*) And Bobby Rintrona, so eager to help. Did Bobby believe that lending a hand to Eliot Conte would put him at the head of the line to collect Silvio Conte's gratitude? Or was there something else in Bobby's quickness for involvement? Bobby, whom he barely knew.

At 4:30, Conte goes to the kitchen for his infallible soporific: five tablespoons of peanut butter, a short glass of warm milk, and three ibuprofen. Back in bed he channels his roiling thoughts into an imaginary box the other side of the bedroom, lid locked down and soldered, then commences his version of counting sheep: titles of Melville's novels, in chronological order, and the names and positions of the New York Yankees' twenty-five-man roster. At 9:30 he awakes after five more hours without prostate interference – a total of ten in all since the night before and happy to be feeling healthy and looking reasonably decent for his dinner that evening with Catherine Cruz.

A quick shower, coffee, and ready to hit the road for his hour-and-a-half drive to Troy, to meet Rintrona at noon, when a knock at the door. Sweet-smiling Tom Castellano holding with two hands a large blue cast-iron pot.

"I caught you on the way out, Detective. Hey, I made this for you."

"Tom, how kind. Please come in."

"I have something else too, no matter how trivial, like you said. Have a couple of minutes?"

"I do, Tom, fifteen tops, then I need to leave for the Albany area."

"You need to refrigerate it, Detective. My mother's sauce, may she rest in peace. The recipe goes back from our mother to her mother's mother and who knows how far. Mine is the unaltered version, unlike Ricky, who had to change it. I asked why change our mother and he comes back with some garbage about individualism. That, if you want to know, was when we went our separate ways. Fuckin' Ricky. I'm wasting your time, Detective."

"Thanks, Tom."

"Enough here for three meals, unless you have guests, which you could use some, I'm thinking."

"Thank you."

They're standing in the kitchen.

"He doesn't pay his rent with a check."

"Jed Kinter?"

"Too trivial, Detective?"

Conte pauses before answering.

"Are you saying he doesn't have a checking account?"

"He has one. Don't ask me how I know."

"He has one but pays the rent in cash?"

"Yep."

"Always?"

"Ever since he moved in three years ago."

Conte says nothing. Did Kinter pay the McPhersons in cash? Must ask Janice.

"Trivial or interesting, Detective?"

"Not trivial, Tom. How much are you charging him?"

"It's a very nice apartment. Nothing better on the East Side, you saw with your own eyes. Six bills a month."

"Thanks, Tom. For the sauce and the info."

"I have something else. His car? A new BMW?"

"Yes?"

"Three years ago he had a different new one then. What I wanta know, Detective, where the fuck does the money come from? This shitty, low-level reporter a new BMW every three years? See what I'm saying?"

"I do, Tom."

"Mulling it over, Detective?"

"You've been helpful, Tom."

"Have a safe trip, Detective, better Albany than here, if you ask me, after what happened last night."

Conte looks at him blankly.

"You didn't hear about it?"

"What?"

"The brutal murder."

"No."

"A woman bludgeoned to death in her own home. Face beyond recognition. Naked and wounded in the vagina with semen on display. Over in south Utica. Chestnut Street."

Conte steps in close to Castellano. Castellano steps back.

"What's her name, Tom? Do you recall?"

Steps in closer. Castellano steps back.

"Janice McPherson."

With sudden violent abruptness, Conte picks up Castellano and holds him high against the wall.

"Whoa! Detective!"

"Don't tell me what you told me. This is a warning. Don't tell me what you just told me."

"Please, Detective, I only repeated."

Just as abruptly, Conte sets Castellano down. Walks over to the kitchen table and sits. Castellano frozen at the wall. Face in hands, Conte says, "I know her. Can you forgive me?"

A long pause.

"You know her?"

"Yes."

"A friend?"

"Do they have a suspect? Can you forgive me, Tom?"

"No suspect. Hey! No harm, no foul. What happened just now, it didn't happen. It was too quick to be real. Hope you like the sauce."

On the way out, Castellano, in a cold sweat, stops briefly at Conte's desk and stares down at the blow-ups.

Conte exits the Thruway at Schenectady, finds a liquor store, asks for a fifth of Johnnie Walker Black. When the clerk returns to the register with the bottle, Conte is gone. At 11:55 he pulls into the parking lot of the Q Shack. A minute later, a car pulls up beside him – Rintrona, who has arranged through Catherine Cruz to be let into the private office, where they sit now with their sandwiches and lemonade. Rintrona also has an order of hush puppies. Rintrona eats, Conte does not, gives Rintrona all the details, talking rapidly – his questions and puzzlements, his paranoia, the grief and guilt for Nelson Thomas and Janice McPherson – saying, at the end of his story, that the key may be Coca. Break him down, we get to the bottom of it all, the spider at the center.

Rintrona says nothing. Working on his sandwich and hush puppies. Eating and nodding. Even after Conte has finished speaking, he nods. Wipes his mouth. Drinks long from his sixteen ounce cup of lemonade:

"That it, Eliot? Anything more you'd like to divulge?"

"Are you ready to help with Coca?"

"What exactly do you want me to do?"

"Did you acquire the chloral hydrate?"

"In the car. With the fuckin' clown mask."

"I don't see Catherine until 7:00. In between now and then, I'll take a room at the Super 8 motel, not far from here, where I intend to spend the afternoon – resting and writing out the scenario. Could you stop by at 6:30 to pick up your copy?"

"The clown mask. My copy of the scenario. Love the mystery. Okay. Listen. Here's a few things in response to your story. No offense: I've been a real detective for years and there's something I know which you, from your questions, I'm thinking you're naïve. In the pursuit of a serious crimi-nal, in this case extreme serious, there are cockteasing loose ends. You constantly think, if only I could tie those all up I would know everything there is to know and bring down all the ancillary bastards too. Total fuckin' knowledge. But these loose ends can't be tied up. Ever. You don't get laid. No harmonious story awaits your brilliance that once you put it all together you never have to think about it again. You never stop thinking about who you didn't bring to justice on this wretched earth. The only thing you can be sure of is you nailed your killer and some lawyer whose morals are worse than a terrorist's can't subvert the evidence. The truth of the evidence is your only truth. Forget this Polack and why he lied about Whitaker and Kinter being gay for each other. Forget this Donny and why Kinter showed up to see him while you were there. Donny is irrelevant. Whitaker is involved, but I doubt as a major force. I could be wrong. I'm often wrong. Coca must be broken down. Of course. He must be reduced. I agree. Your friend the chief of police is dirty. How dirty? We'll see. Coca will tell us after we work him over. Enzo? Don't make me laugh. Strictly speaking, we don't know if Nelson what's-his-name and Judy what's-her-face were murdered thanks to you stepping in where angels fear to butt in. My guess is you were the innocent facilitator. Who killed these poor slobs? Kinter's visitor? Who also did the assassinations? This picture here – look! Not only the shoes, but the suit jacket. It's obvious. Built up in the shoulders by a bad tailor. The man inside the suit and shoes is smaller than he looks. My theory? Kinter and the visitor are the same person. This is a Mafia thing from the beginning."

"Kinter killed Janice?"

"Because she could finger him. Maybe. Maybe Kinter killed her. But didn't you tell me Judy was raped?"

"Janice."

"Whatever. Mafiosi are not historically known for doing a hit and getting ass at the same time from the person they hit."

"Who killed Nelson Thomas?"

"Not Kinter unless he knows Nelson was a witness. Aren't you going to eat, big fella?"

"Who then?"

Before Rintrona can respond, Conte answers his own question: "Robinson has the most to lose."

"Maybe. But everything you tell me about him he's a pussy. Do pussymen kill? On occasion. Coca you say was in the van. He has something definitive, which is why the chief wants you to neutralize him."

"Why won't Robinson neutralize him himself?"

"No idea."

Conte pushes aside his untouched lunch.

"You hardly know me, Bobby, but you're eager to jump into a situation that could cost you your job and pension and maybe more. Because you're in awe of my father? And believe he'll be grateful that you lent me assistance? Hard to swallow."

"At the end of the day? When the fuckin' cows come home? No. There's something maybe in it for me having nothing to do with Silvio Conte. Something potentially very nice. My contact in the FBI has a theory about the triple assassination. He tells me Aristarco was the target, not the Barbones who were gravy. Okay. Aristarco headed one of the classic five families. You know this. He took over for Big Paulie Castellano. Recall him? Gunned down in the early '80s with his driver, outside of Spark's steak house on 46th Street. One of the two button men in trench coats and fedoras was Frank Barbone, who did the job on Aristarco's behalf, who was sick of listening to Big Paulie's constant complaints about his constipation, when is this tall fuck ever going to die of so-called natural causes? That's one filament in the spider's web. The other one is Aristarco's attempt to usurp the drug business of the Patriarca family of Providence. For his greed, Aristarco was supposed to be whacked in a barber's chair at Grand Central, but it didn't happen. A loose end. So Raymond Patriarca looks for another opportunity and when it comes it's too good to be true. A cemetery in Utica, nice small town, bush-league and easily corruptible police. So Patriarca sends one of his people, the so-called visitor, Kinter himself, who ever since lives a civilian life with monthly cold-cash gifts from Providence, a new BMW every three years – he's a vicious family man in deep cover. The Barbones are viewed as extremists within the top levels of Cosa Nostra. They whacked three civilian relatives of one of their enforcer nephews – *just in case*. While you're at it, get rid of these two fuckin' Utica animals who bring us bad publicity, that's Kinter's directive. We break this case, Eliot – we get book offers. Big advances for each of us in seven figures. We get TV appearances. We get live internet streaming of our daily lives. We get consultantships on a movie starring Leonardo DiCaprio, who we get to know as Leo, who plays Kinter, with Meryl Streep as Jeanine McPherson, directed by Martin Scorsese, who insists we call him Marty."

"Who plays us?"

"Pacino and Brando."

"Brando is dead."

"WHAT?!"

"Synakowski has the same fantasy. We become rich and famous in a minor sort of way."

"They want to give me minor, Eliot? I take it."

Between 1:30 and 6:30, Conte in the foetid air of the Super 8 naps and works on the scenario. Sketches the set, the blocking, roughs in the dialogue, suggests themes for improvisation, describes the costumes, stipulates acts to be performed with the key props. He's regained his health. He's never felt better. It excites him to work the scenario.

At 6:30 sharp, Rintrona at the door. Takes one look at

Conte and says, "You look like a new man since lunch. They say this is the meaning of falling in love. I wouldn't know. Against all odds, Katie's got a thing for you, you lucky bastard. Here's what you need for Coca's drink."

Conte invites him in. Rintrona sits on the bed as Conte paces, a little manic, a manila folder in hand, paper-clipped at the open edges. He says, "Look this over for tomorrow. We meet at my house at 6:30. We change in the car. No need to memorize. Make it part of you. Make the character you and all else follows."

Rintrona rises, takes the folder, and startles Conte by saying, "In the Program we have a saying, I'm referring to AA, but I'm not telling you you're a candidate. I only observe you're wound tight like a white knuckler. The saying is an acronym. KISS. Keep It Simple Stupid. KISS is also wisdom for detectives. At lunch you mentioned forty-seven confusing characters."

"Did I mention Ronald Sheehan?"

"Number forty-eight."

"Attended DePellaccio in the hospital. An esteemed physician with honorary degrees. He died in a one-car accident a few months after DePellaccio's so-called heart attack."

"Another victim of conspiracy?"

"I believe so."

"Only two people matter, Eliot, who we come down on like a ton of jagged bricks. In private, without pain-in-the-ass witnesses. Coca and Kinter. That's it. Keep it simple and I'll see you *domani*."

"One other thing, Bobby."

"Yeah?"

"The fox knows many things, but the hedgehog knows one big thing."

"What I'm saying."

———————

She's in form-fitting black leather pants and a long-sleeved, low-necked top whose design and vivid color very few women can wear to advantage. Catherine Cruz is one of the very few. She apologizes for having to get take-out from the Thai Café. Planned to cook, but another one of those extended and bruising conversations with her daughter knocked her for a loop.

He says, "Our kids... I sympathize."

"For some reason, Eliot, unhappy encounters tend to whet my appetite. A psychiatrist could have a field day with me. Are you famished?"

"I am." (Allowing himself to think "for you too.")

A spread of crispy catfish, wonton soup, steamed rice, and basil rolls, which they'll dip in a spicy hot sweet sauce. She says, "The dessert they make, which I foolishly bought, will destroy us both."

"Good," he says.

She offers him a Thai beer. He politely declines.

"This fine wine, then?"

"Might you have a Coke? Water is okay too."

"Coke it is."

Unlike their first date at the Q Shack, which went as if they'd known each other long before, this one is awkward – this second meeting is burdened by the knowledge of how much, so quickly, had been felt, and frankly exchanged, at the Q Shack, and now here they are in her studio apartment with a sweeping view of the Hudson, just the two of them, and the sense of intimacy and the pressure of what now? What next?

She says, "Have fun at lunch with Bobby?"

"He's something else, Catherine, isn't he?"

"A constant entertainment and the most devoted family guy I've met. When Bobby returned, he said, Katie, I'm the canary that just swallowed the cat." (Fishing.)

Conte tells her a truth of a preliminary sort that won't be questioned. "He's advising me on a delicate case."

"Very mysterious, Detective Conte. Mystery is good. Anticipation is good too, up to a point. I hope it goes well for you."

"We'll see."

"We'll see is what anticipation is all about, isn't it?"

Not to be outdone, he responds in kind to her code: "Both the pleasure and the agony. I've always known the agony as a big part of the pleasure."

Conte and Cruz forget themselves for a moment, lay aside their troubles, and the dinner and conversation become ever more delectable, until over coffee and coconut cake he tells her that at the Q Shack he had misled her about his children, when he told her that he and they were irreversibly alienated. He's sorry he didn't level with her.

"In fact, Catherine, they're dead."

She can't respond.

He says, "Do you watch CNN by any chance?"

"For about an hour after dinner."

"Recall a story out of California last week abo
arrested on suspicion of murdering her adult chil

She doesn't want to answer. After a long paus

"That was my ex, those were her. My girls. Rosalind and
Emily. I haven't seen them since I moved east twenty years
ago."

He leaves the table, walks to the window, stares at the
river.

"They're gone. She's been released."

She joins him at the window. His voice is lifeless.

"I don't believe she did it. What's the difference who
did?... What's the difference?... Where's the satisfaction in
knowing who? What good will it do me?"

She takes his hand, but doesn't speak.

"I thought for the longest time I felt nothing for them
because of – what's the point of going over the marriage
and the separation? The coldness from the beginning. The
bitterness that came too quickly. The actual hatred at the
end and damages not even God, if there is one, could re-
deem. Now this, thirty years later. I'm empty. That's who I
am. I totally failed. No chance now to give the love they
shouldn't have had to earn, and never got from me. God is not
interested."

She turns his head toward her. He embraces her. He
steps back. Not wanting to feel what he's suddenly feeling.

He says, "I need to get back. Big day tomorrow."

She says, "Are you free on Saturday?"

"Yes."

"I'd like to come up to Utica."

"We could listen to the opera in the afternoon, then go

to The Chesterfield for dinner. The owners are friends of mine. Rosie and Dom. They'd love to meet you."

He turns toward the window: "There's your river, Catherine."

"After dinner at The Chesterfield, unless you object, I won't drive home. I'll stay."

"What are we saying the meaning of 'stay' is?"

"Sleep in your bed."

At the door, she says, "I want you to do something."

He looks at her.

"Put your hands on my breasts."

He does.

He says, "Will this help?"

"Yes," she says. "Yes."

CHAPTER 18

Conte over the speed limit, near Schenectady, enters the Mohawk Valley's mouth – down its long throat he goes – all the way down to the bottom of the belly at exit 33, Utica at last, where he tunes in to WIBX and a bulletin of the latest news: "An anonymous police source is reporting tonight that a neighbor of Janice McPherson has come forward to say that while walking his dog on Chestnut Street, between 8:30 and 9:00 P.M., he recalls a large man entering the murder victim's house. Unfortunately, our source stated, it was too dark and at too great a distance for the witness to notice anything other than the man's impressive size."

If the neighbor's estimate is accurate – if the large man can be placed at the scene within a time frame ultimately corroborated by the coroner – then Janice's son will testify as to Conte's urgent interest in seeing the mother – witnesses at the college will testify that he'd been to her office a few days before – one of them will claim to have overheard heated conversation as she strolled past the victim's door – and then, inevitably, he thinks, the dog-walker's description of a large man entering her house at the fatal time becomes damning. Dr. Jekyll, allow me the pleasure of introducing you to Mr. Hyde.

Home at 11:30 – the light flashing on his answering machine. Two messages. The first at 10:05:

El, Toots. Your father was taken to Saint Elizabeth's about an hour ago by ambulance. He called from his room. Antonio's with him. I hate to say it, but it doesn't look too good at this point, but maybe not the worst, God willing. El, I, uh, hope you'll get over to the hospital first thing in the morning. If not tonight. He wants to see you very much, believe me. It's time, El.

The second at 10:20:

Detective Conte, it's Tom. I saw something that reminded me of something in those blow-up pictures on your desk this morning. I couldn't place it at the time. The mouth. I just placed it. The tiny no-lips mouth. Why my tenant is wearing a wig and moustache I have no idea, but I'm betting you do. Tomorrow morning, after he goes to work, I intend to investigate his storage in the attic. You looked into the suitcase. I'm looking into his fuckin' boxes. You never know. I'll be in touch.

In spite of the hour's lateness, Conte returns Castellano's call and gets his answering machine:

Tom, please take this very seriously. Jed Kinter is extremely dangerous. Let's talk first thing in the

morning. Don't do anything crazy. Do nothing until
we talk.

Conte sleeps no more than an hour, if that. At 7:00 he calls
Castellano, gets the man himself, and apologizes for calling at
such an hour. Castellano replies, "You call 7:00 in the morning early? You got some kind of lifestyle, Detective." Conte
warns him that Kinter has likely done multiple murders –
"stay out of his way – be careful how you look at him – say
you're coming down with a cold, or whatever, if you run into
him – try to act bored in his presence."

Castellano replies, "Christ, I'm always bored. Listen to
this: I already did my investigation while Kinter slept. 3:00
in the morning, Detective, I'm up in the attic on catlike
feet. Guess what? I found built-up shoes and a revolver. The
fuckin' shorty kept the shoes."

"Jesus Christ, Tom."

"I confiscated the fuckin' revolver."

"You're out of your mind."

"And you're not, Detective?"

"Does he usually eat at home and stick around in the
evenings?"

"Sometimes he's here, mostly he's not. Tonight, he'll definitely be here."

"How do you know that?"

"How do I know? Last night I invited this bastard for
dinner. That's how I know."

"He accepted?"

"Naturally."

"Naturally?? How long do you think he'll stay?"

"As long as it takes."

"What are you saying to me, Tom?"

"I'm saying he'll be here from six to fuckin' indefinite. In other words, whenever you can get here, Detective, to do what you have to do."

"What are you telling me, Tom?"

"I'm telling you I guarantee it, Detective."

"Don't do anything crazy, Tom."

"This fuckin' guy, Detective? Ever since he came here three years ago, he acts like I'm his father. I think he's got some kind of perversity about Italian men of a certain age. We have a nice relationship."

"I'll come over after seven or eight. I'll call in advance."

"No need to call. Just come."

"Tom, you're really beginning to scare me."

"About time, Detective, don't ya think?"

———————

He approaches Silvio Conte's private room as a nurse exits. He stops her, she glares: "Excuse me, Teresa, what can you tell me about the seriousness of my father's condition?"

Teresa, once a knockout who has added twenty-five pounds to her diminutive frame, responds: "I look like a doctor to you?"

"As a matter of fact, I think you – "

"Nice try."

As she pushes past, he says, "He's my father. He *is* my father, Teresa."

She gives him an incredulous look: "Years ago, as we all know, he semi-adopted a black child, who has since risen to glory. And we all hear the rumors he fathered a daughter out of wedlock. As far as I can tell, you're not black. I'm calling security."

"Let me show you my ID."

"Passport or drivers'. No credit cards."

Arms akimbo, she stares at his drivers'.

"Who knew? Mr. Conte, as I declared, I'm not a so-called doctor and can't ethically give you medical information. Follow me, but not too closely."

She takes him to a deserted area near the Coke machine. She whispers:

"Congestive heart failure. It's obviously been going on for years. Or don't you notice your father's health status?"

"The prognosis?"

"He has end-stage symptoms."

"How much time does he have?"

"Do I look like God to you?"

"I never saw God."

"You have a mouth on you, Mr. Eliot Conte."

"Sorry."

"Never fails. After forty years in this job, they can't stop themselves from joking around near the dying and even to the dying. Who knows? Maybe it does everyone some good, including the ones on their way out. You heard nothing from me, Mr. Conte. I lose my job in this economy?"

"One more thing."

"You're insatiable."

"A *passport?*"

"These days they come from all over. Mr. Conte, Utica is globalized."

"Thanks, Teresa."

"For what?"

Donatella Tomasi sits on the bed. Father Gustavo stands, swaying a little, one foot to the other. In an armchair upholstered and cushioned in the Italian tricolors – brought by his Mexican assistant – Big Daddy is at rest. Legs crossed. Not hooked up to an IV – or anything else. Not dressed in a hospital gown. Instead he's flamboyant in one of his tailor-made Italian suits (his single indulgence), tan and pinstriped, with a flowered tie. Big Daddy is the son plus thirty-three years. Once two inches taller and much heavier in solid muscle, he's now gone skeletal and gaunt-faced: flesh receded, cheekbones thrust forward. Emaciated except for the last-stage symptom of the abdomen – six months pregnant there. Big Daddy is big with gaudy death.

Eliot enters and his father is overtaken: "My son is here." He struggles to his feet, falls back into his chair, struggles again to rise, succeeds, waving off his son's assistance. They embrace. Silvio warmly, relaxed – Eliot awkward, stiff.

Silvio says, "Assist me to my chair, if you don't mind, Eliot." Eliot helps him back down.

"Thank you. I'm afraid to sit down too hard. The bones."

"How are you, Dad?" (Standing by the father.)

Silvio, pointing to Father Gustavo: "He's come to

administer what he calls Last Rites. I prefer to call it Extreme Unction. I enjoy the old-time words. This is a thing" – catching his failing breath – "my son and I have a common pleasure in, the sounds of words, don't we, Eliot?"

"Yes."

"Extreme Unction."

Father G responds, wagging his finger: "My dear Silvio, this is the eighth time in the last five years that I've performed this sad ritual on your behalf and here you are, and here I am again, and I look forward to rendering this melancholy service eight more times at a minimum."

Tootsie says, "*Cent'anni*! Silvio."

Silvio replies, "This beautiful woman, who reminds me of her mother, thinks every day is my birthday."

"Something wrong with that, Big Daddy?" Tootsie says.

Looking at his son: "What's your opinion, Eliot?"

"*Cent'anni*, Dad, in advance of tomorrow, your actual birthday."

"Oh, my God! I forgot!" says Tootsie.

"And I?" says Father G. "I'm in the dark, as usual."

Silvio's breath failing, a brief cough. "I never knew that I wanted anymore to know such a thing," breath failing again, "until my son here just wished for me a hundred more."

Eliot nods, pats his father's shoulder. Silvio places his hand over Eliot's, as Eliot begins to caress Silvio's shoulder – intimacy virtually unknown to them since Eliot's childhood. It occurs to each, simultaneously, that it may be forced (it isn't) because the occasion – the father's imminent death, the long-alienated son's last-minute affection – triggers self-consciousness and feelings of falsity for both, how could it be otherwise? Though less, much less, for the father than the son.

Tootsie needs to get to the bank. Father G has promised to lead the meeting of the parish theological book club, whose membership is wholly (blessedly, he thinks) comprised of women. Tootsie and Father G are grateful to have excuses to leave, having witnessed this moment of father and son. They imagine reconciliation at last.

"Have to go to work, Silvio. See you later." She kisses him and he has memories of Angie Tomasi.

He replies, "*Speriamo che sì*." (We hope so.)

Father G, "I'll be back this afternoon."

Tootsie's gone. Father G is halted at the door by Silvio's mischievous, "Be careful of the pretty women! Or should I say, the pretty women need to be careful of The Great Cuban," failing breath, coughing, "Lover?"

Father G replies, "Formerly. Ages ago."

Silvio says, "I believe her name is Marina, that sexy Russian?"

"You're bad, Silvio."

"Yes, Father, we are." Father Gustavo leaves.

Eliot and his father are alone. Silvio breaks the silence: "No more beating around the bush, is there?"

"I don't know what to say."

"How about, this is our last chance? The arrhythmia is almost out of control. A massive stroke waits for me around the corner. I cough blood. It's not that I can't pee because of the prostate – the problem is my body wishes to preserve my urine in ridiculous places. Look at my ankles! Swollen with poison."

"I'm sorry, Dad."

"Who has the time for sorry or self-pity?"

"Neither of us."

"We're on the same page, Eliot."

"Really?"

"We were always on the same page."

He stares at his father.

"Think I belong in the crazy house for saying that?"

"Afraid I do."

"We've both been lousy fathers. That's the page."

"What can I say?"

"Agree or not?"

"I agree."

"Please pull up that uncomfortable chair. Come a little closer. Thank you."

"You're welcome."

"Let's be extremely blunt: When your kids were babies, you left them. I never left, but I wasn't there for you and it had nothing to do with Antonio. Nothing. Stop torturing yourself with that thought. Think I don't know?" Brief cough, then a second, more sustained. "It had to do with my political life, which crowded out everything. My political life was my irresistible and illicit woman. She ate up all my time."

Eliot rises and looms over his father: "Don't give me that shit! You found time every third week of every August to go fishing with your pals up to the Saint Lawrence River. Except you never said the Saint Lawrence River. It was always 'The River.' The words were magical. 'The River.' I imagined, and still do, the two of us there, in that enchanted place, but it never happened and never will. That's what I need. Not the fucking house on Mary Street. Goddamn you! Blunt enough for you, Dad?"

"At fifty-five years old, you still need your father so much?"

Eliot, in a monotone: "Don't play dumb. After you're dead, I'll still be a son who needs his father."

"Is that why you abandoned your kids?"

"What?"

"Give unto your children what was given unto you? Almost nothing? Your children are dead and you're alive. This is the problem. Your children no longer have the pain of losing their daddy. What are the words for such pain as you gave when you abandoned them for the wife of the provost of UCLA? As I abandoned you. We're still here, Eliot," sustained coughing, choking on phlegm. "I have a week or two, maybe. Shall we? No? Yes? You'll think about it? Shall we take a chance? Don't think about it too long."

"I never told you or anyone else it was the provost's wife. How the hell do you know that?"

"You asked the provost to give his wife a divorce. He said something to you and you did that crazy thing that you did."

"How the hell do you know all that?"

"From my friend, the original Big Daddy – Jesse Unruh himself, may he rest in peace, who ran the Democratic party in California. One of the great old-style political bosses, greater than Richard Daley – Jesse had his fingers up everything. The original Big Daddy was very big and he was your best friend in California, which you never knew. Know what he said about the University of California you were so proud of? A pimple on the ass of the state."

"You knew him? Jesse Unruh?"

"Democratic convention 1960, when we nominated JFK in Los Angeles. The first Big Daddy and I spent a lot of time together in consultation with Bobby, drinks and sandwiches and cigars in the middle of the night and Jack checking in once in a while to tease his younger brother, how we were going to ward off LBJ."

"You devised strategy with Bobby Kennedy? You never told me. How come?"

"I'm telling you now. Try to accept me now. In those days, we had only a couple of these stupid primaries, where they spend millions to convince the ignorant. They didn't spend millions back then because it was mostly done by the big bosses."

"You were a really big boss. Still are."

"Thank you. The first Big Daddy threw California to JFK and that made him almost unstoppable. Almost. My own role, I was at the tender age of thirty-three already the big boss of upstate New York. The Democrats up here were scared of nominating a Catholic, not to mention the Italians had a hard time forgetting what the Irish did to them when we came over. Downstate delegates were in Jack's pocket. I got him upstate and that gave him New York and California. Illinois and Pennsylvania followed our lead, and the nomination and then the presidency and then Dallas. That's the favor we did him. November twenty-second, 1963. We were in so many words helping to take his life. (My breath is coming back pretty good now.) They wanted him dead and they got their wish."

"Who wanted him dead, Dad? Who are 'they'?"

"Talk about an electric personality? I shook his hand in Los Angeles and I thought I was getting electrocuted."

"You shook his hand?"

"I'm changing this bitter subject."

"Okay. Back to the original Big Daddy. Tell me the story."

"At the time Big Jesse and I met, the boys in upstate used to call me The Machine. I didn't care for it. Sounded inhuman. So when I got back, I told them from now on refer to me with affection as Big Daddy. Jesse called to tell me about your troubles. The police out there had you in custody, think I don't know? You were going down for a very long count. The original Big Daddy made it all go away."

"How did he do it, Big Daddy?"

"Say it with more affection."

"Big Daddy?"

"That's an improvement. I reached out to him and he reached out on your behalf – this is all we need to know."

"Politics."

"I call it love."

"You're kidding, right?"

"Taking care of one another? That's not what love is? What else could it be?"

Eliot says nothing.

"Taking care of people in need, isn't that it? That's how I showed it to you, getting you the house, even though I never took you to The River."

"Politics – so many cruel bastards who only take care of the wealthy."

"That's true. But I got involved because Utica's biggest minority group, the Italian people, were getting the short end. And they were getting it rammed you know where. I changed that. I made mayors. Police chiefs. I got them city jobs. I got their modest homes *properly* revalued for lower taxes. I got their streets fixed and plowed equally to the rich people up on the Parkway. I got their kids summer jobs supervising the playgrounds. I got an Italian boy, a black boy, and a Polish boy into West Point. I got a Lebanese into the Naval Academy. I went to a lot of wakes and funerals, Eliot. I showed up when they were very happy and I showed up when they were very sad."

"And they gave you their votes."

"Don't make it sound dirty. They repaid my love with theirs in the only way they could. One hand washes the other. With votes, they voted. All the while, I didn't love you well."

"If I hadn't left my kids, they'd be alive – I have blood on my hands, you don't."

"That's a tough idea to reject if you think life is all about if."

"What's it all about, Big Daddy?"

"I'm not hearing it with enough affection yet. Eliot, I never dealt in what's-it-all-about speculation. Doesn't put bread on anyone's table."

"You still live in that rickety old two-family house on Catherine Street that your parents lived in. You never took a piece of the pie. You bought and made over for me a house much better than your own. Guilt of the absentee father?"

"Who knows? Who cares? The result, that's what counts. My breath is coming good now. Have you noticed? If I improve, listen, if I improve a little more in the coming days, I know a special place on The River, where we fish together for big northern pike – three, four feet long with teeth like razors! Watch out, El, he'll take your hand off!"

"Out of season?"

"We were always that, son. Why stop now?"

"The game warden will have our ass."

"That would be Alex Thompson. I got his wife's punitive divorce settlement reduced in half."

"In other words?"

"Politics, Eliot."

"Love."

"Now we're cooking with gas!"

"How are you feeling, Dad? I mean right now."

"Better."

"Physically, you mean."

"The mental way too. How about you?"

"I got very little sleep last night."

"I mean the mental way, El."

"Do I have to answer?"

"Don't we feel better the mental way too? Just a little?"

"I'll be back after lunch. Before I go, though, I could use some insider information on Sanford Whitaker."

"You won't say you feel better too?"

"No. Not now."

"If I were you, I wouldn't either."

"Sorry, I can't. Not now."

"After I'm gone, I hope you won't go too negative against yourself because of us."

"Maybe I'll deserve to go negative. Maybe you were doing the best you could. Nobody should ask more of anyone. (Pause.) We ask anyway."

"Maybe we were both dealt bad cards in the family game. I think I feel more energy in my legs. Do I seem better, El?"

"You actually do. This Whitaker, Dad. He writes vicious editorials on you twice a month for as long as I've been back, but I have the suspicion he's dirty in a matter that interests me."

"I'll make it short so you can get some rest. At the beginning, years ago, maybe thirty-five years back, he came into the *O.D.* hierarchy on a mission to destroy me. Then one summer night, you were still out in California, one of Utica's finest in plain clothes, a *paesan*, Don Belmont, caught him propositioning an underage girl. Thirteen years old. Naturally, the detective, while he still has him cuffed in the car, gives me a call from a pay phone about nailing this stone in my shoe. I tell the detective to hold off until I give the go-ahead. Put him on the phone. I say to Whitaker, I can make this go away. I can get your property tax reduced to a dollar a year and your utility bills to disappear. He says to me, Mr. Conte – I say don't call me that. Say Big Daddy and say it like you like me. He says, Big Daddy, I'll never write a critical editorial about you again. Sanford, I say, I want you to keep writing those editorials, but make them even more vicious because since you came to town your editorial writing has solidified, and deepened, my support in this fair city. Do you agree? Good. And if I ever hear you doing a disgusting proposition again, I go directly to Jerry Fiore at WKTV. I had the detective write a letter, notarized, concerning Whitaker's sexual taste. A copy of this document was delivered to Whitaker."

"You own Whitaker."

"I don't believe in slavery."

"Whitaker is your creature."

"You have a way with words, son."

"I'll see you later today."

"I look forward."

"Bye, Dad."

Eliot moves to the door. His father is seized by a violent fit of coughing. Eliot freezes at the door, turns, but cannot go to his father. The cough is ceaseless. When at last Eliot takes a step in his father's direction, Silvio's white shirt, tie, and pants are sprayed with bloody mucus. Eliot freezes again, staring. Eliot goes to his father's side. The coughing stops. Silvio spits, chokes, slumps over.

"Dad?"

Silvio, who rarely curses, mumbles, weakly, "Any idea what I shelled out for these fucking… clothes? Help me to the bed. Please… this way, with my arm over your shoulders… pick up my arm… thank you… stand on my own now… hoist me… I walk on my own if you hold… can't… can't do it." At which point, Eliot picks his father up and carries him, like a child in his arms, his father's head resting on Eliot's chest, to bed.

"I'll get you a change of clothes."

"The nurse."

"I'll do it."

"The nurse."

"I'll call the nurse."

Big Daddy summons what's left of his disappearing strength: "The son should never undress the father."

CHAPTER 19

The door's ajar and a man of impressive size sits again at Conte's desk with *Moby-Dick*: "This fucker could write, El. Listen to this: A damp, drizzly November in my soul. Describes you to a tee. Maybe me."

"You shouldn't be anywhere near me today, Robby."

"November the first and it's drizzling on my assistant chief's D-Day."

"Better get over to the hospital. He could go any minute."

"I'm on the way. He was bad last night. You just see him?"

"Yes. He's very bad."

"So why aren't you there?"

"As if you didn't know. What time does our friend leave the station?"

"Around 5:15 – 5:30."

"Make sure he stays until then. Denise and Millicent in New York, I trust?"

"I'm trustable, El."

"After tonight our friend is safe."

"How about me, El? Am I safe?"

"I need sleep, Robby. Better go now."

"Call me after."

"Count on it. Go to Silvio."

"Coca's gonna lie through his teeth, El."

"You're a man of quite impressive size, Robby."

Antonio doesn't respond.

"Go to him, who art not in Heaven."

———————————

3:45 P.M. He's had two hours of dead sleep.

Conte changes the license plate on his car, in his drive-way. Out of sight. In the car, puts on his costume. Ten min-utes later, the same car pulls up to a well-kept, single-family house on Sherman Drive. A man in coveralls and a large floppy hat pulled low emerges, goes to the trunk, removes a garden hose and shovel, walks to the back of the residence, where expertly and quickly he opens the door, enters, finds a bottle of Campari about two-thirds full in the dining area, unscrews the top, pours something in through a small funnel, secures the top and shakes gently, then departs, expertly and quickly locking the door from the outside. Leaves the hose but takes the shovel. The car pulls into the driveway at 1318 Mary Street, where the man removes the costume in the car, enters the house at 4:17.

———————————

5:30. He hasn't eaten all day, but has no appetite. An hour early, carrying a shopping bag, Rintrona arrives. They sit in the kitchen. Conte has prepared a sandwich of salami and pro-volone for Rintrona, who had announced his hunger upon arrival. Conte sips a cup of his favorite tea.

"This is the craziest operation I've been involved in. Great salami! You think this guy is going to cough up something that'll crack the triple assassination? Don't we already have the obvious suspect in mind? This Kinter. He's the fuckin' doer, got to be. Why do we do a job on this Coca?"

Conte tells him what Castellano has uncovered and Rintrona replies, "So, okay, let's come down on Kinter and forget about Coca."

"We can't forget Coca – he might be the key to a conspiracy of some breadth. Who killed DePellaccio? Ronald Sheehan? Nelson Thomas? Who killed Janice McPherson?"

"Kinter is the leading and probably only candidate, all due respect. Sheehan? Thomas? On those two you might be talking out of your et cetera, all due respect. Accidental more likely with those two. McFarlane? A sex killer. Kinter is a sex killer on top of everything else? You working on a bad movie? DePellaccio? Okay, I buy DePellaccio, if Kinter gave him the bribe. But only if. We add them up on your theory, Kinter did seven since he came to Utica to open a slaughterhouse, for Chrissake."

"I have a feeling that seven is accurate."

"You have a *feeling*? From what part of your body does it emanate?"

"I take your point, Bobby."

"On the basis of your feeling, let's say you're right. Okay. Kinter's paid to do three hits on three Mafia heavies. That we can take to the bank. What's the motivation to do the others? Mafia hitmen do not hit civilians. In the history of these scumbags, I know of no deliberate civilian hits. Maybe here and there an accidental innocent bystander."

"Unless there's something involved that's not Mafia-related. Mafia plus X."

"What would that be?"

"I don't know."

"Raymond Patriarca, Mr. Detective Conte, got what he wanted with the elimination of Aristarco. The Barbones were gravy, as we discussed. Okay. DePellaccio maybe could identify the hitman, okay, if the hitter did the bribe personally, which I doubt because doing bribes is entrusted to non-hitters, like lawyers usually. I don't buy your theory. Your theory doesn't touch facts. So where are we, *paesan*?"

"We put the squeeze on Coca and do whatever we need to do to Kinter's body, but without crossing the line, and see what that yields."

"In this kind of event, Eliot, it's good to bring the equalizer. I'm packing a .38 special. What d'you have?"

".357 Magnum."

"A blessing upon you. You carrying it to the festivities?"

"Yes."

"We can only pray to our Virgin Mother that one of us gets pushed over the edge. I forecast you."

6:00. Conte and Rintrona in street clothes drive in the car with the changed plate to the house on Sherman Drive. The street is deserted. Rintrona gets out, walks rapidly to the front door, knocks. No answer. Rings doorbell. No answer. Presses bell repeatedly, finally leaning on it. Nothing. Walks behind front hedge and peers in. Turns to Conte, who's still in the car, and smiles, then returns to tell him that a man with an obvious toupee is stretched out on the couch. A glass on the floor beside him, turned over. Conte sneer-smiles. Seeing that the street is still deserted, Conte and Rintrona, each carrying a shopping bag, walk rapidly in the full dark to the back door and enter.

6:23. Rintrona closes the door, pulls the drapes, turns off all lighting in the house with the exception of a small, low-wattage lamp, which he places on the coffee table fronting the couch, where the man known with scorn as Michael C lies in profound sleep. Conte and Rintrona proceed carefully to haul the man to the floor. Blindfold him with a black cloth. Strip him naked. Handcuff him wrists to ankles. And, last, with the utmost of delicate precision, do something to the man with a lubricated dildo of modest size.

Thinking of himself as a priest conducting a baptismal ceremony, Rintrona pours a glass of cold water on the head of Michael C, who groans but does not come to. A second glass. Again he groans, awakes, falls back asleep. A handkerchief soaked in ammonia, pressed to the nostrils. Violent head snap – he awakes, screaming, but will not be heard because Pavarotti at high volume is singing "Di quella pira," the heroic call to arms from *Il Trovatore*. A voice close to Coca's ear. The voice says the music must be turned off for purposes of "penetrating conversation," and should Coca scream in the ensuing quietude "feel this against your cheek?"

"Yes."

Music off.

"Open your mouth." The cold barrel of a .38 inserted.

"Close your mouth. Good. Feel good? Answer me, darling."

Coca nods, whimpers.

"Do we understand one another?"

Coca nods.

"How the *fuck* could it feel good, asshole, to have a .38 in your mouth? You cunt. But I really do understand why you'd think it wise to nod in the affirmative. I really do. Can't be too careful with our answers, can we, sweetheart? Don't answer. Good. This'll go easily for everybody, especially for your honorable guests, and perhaps you, as well, depending. Depending. Feel something firm in your – I can't say the word because my mother, may she rest in peace, will wash my mouth out with soap. She'll pierce my naughty tongue with a hot needle. How could you not appreciate what you feel in your?" Rintrona laughs quietly. "Stupid question? Yes? Be careful. Answer with maximum care. Because I'm sick of your lies. Prepared for a viewing?"

Coca nods.

"Goody! Goody goody gumdrops! When I remove the blindfold keep your eyes shut tight until I tell you to open them. Be a good bitch and the chances of survival are fifty-fifty. Suppress the urge to scream when I tell you to open those peepers or your chances of survival are one in forty-three point three. Open your eyes."

Michael C in a mental scream: Mouth open wide without sound. Standing about five feet away, a short rotund man, in a happy-face rubber clown mask that covers his skull, naked except for a pair of jockey shorts artfully stuffed with three pair of socks. A .38 in his right hand, barrel in mouth. Surgical gloves. About ten feet back, in shadow, a figure of impressive size. Black coat to the ankles. Black watch cap low over the forehead and covering his ears. A black cloth covering his face, with eye holes, fluttering with every exhale. White tennis shoes, red laces. Surgical gloves.

Clown mask walks over to the man in black, points to the face covering, says, "Do you know what this is?" Coca shakes his head. "The Minister's Black Veil, dummy. Do you know who he is?" Coca shakes his head. "The Man of the Crowd." From the pocket of his long coat, the man in black removes a dildo of epic proportions, a fork with sharpened tines protruding from its tip. "Oh, God, please!" Clown mask says, "You blaspheme. I am not God. That, dear Mikey, is your unlubricated destiny, should you not truthfully cooperate. Do you know the meaning of home?" Coca stares. "Home is the place, when you have to go there, they have to take you in. We have come to take you in."

The Man of the Crowd, enforked dildo in hand, walks behind Michael C, kneels, slowly withdraws the secret fantasy of all stout-hearted men, the smaller dildo, then presses his instrument against, but not within. Clown mask says, "Do you renounce Satan and the glamour of evil, from this day forth?" Coca replies, "I won't bother Antonio Robinson from this day forth." Clown mask says, "You bet your bloody ass you won't." Coca in a torrent, "On the van that day, you want me to tell you about the van that day when the light was red and the running nigger had the light in his favor and was going to cross in front of the van when the light

was red, and Robinson what he did I'll tell you about that,
you want me to tell you about that when Robinson who is
driving sees the running nigger he's going to cross in front
of the van because he has the light in his favor and Robinson stiff-arms out the window like a traffic cop, which is
all he ever deserved to be, except Big Daddy, he stiff-arms
to the running nigger like you stop traffic and the nigger
doesn't cross even though he has the light in his favor and
Robinson even though the light is red floors it across the
intersection and broadsides the bus, you want me to tell you
about that he did it on purpose, the driving nigger didn't
want to kill the running nigger because even though the
running nigger had the light the driving nigger knew he
was going to run it, we never get to the cemetery to protect,
they were shot, you want me to tell you about that and I
won't bother Robinson from this day forth? Do you want
me to?" Clown mask says, "This is your last chance. Do you,
or do you not, renounce Satan and the glamour of evil?"
Coca passes out. Ammonia. He revives. Eagerly swallows
the Campari they hold to his mouth in greedy gulps. Goes
under.

Rintrona and Conte haul him to bed. Remove cuffs,
empty the remaining contents of the bottle of Campari, remove their costumes, turn off the small lamp, return it to its
original place and leave. In the car, Conte calls Castellano to
tell him that he's on the way.

Castellano replies, "Don't rush. He's safe."

Rintrona says, "Kinter now?"

"Appears so."

"How did I do, Eliot?"

"Your improvisational powers are considerable. I hardly recognized you, Bobby."

"My work at Troy Little Theater."

"You're an actor?"

"More fun than a barrel of monkeys."

"We won't need costumes for the next one."

"Kinter?"

"Jed."

In civvies, and packing heat, Conte and Rintrona are greeted before they can knock by Castellano holding a glass of red wine. He urges them to make themselves comfortable in the front room, then goes to the kitchen and carries back two glasses and the bottle.

Conte stands, says, in irritation, "You cannot be serious. Where is he, Tom?"

"Who would you be referring to, Detective?"

"Cut it out, Tom."

"Stop fucking with us, Mr. Castellano."

"I thought we'd relax first."

Conte and Rintrona shoot him lethal looks.

Tom says, "Okay, okay."

They follow him into the kitchen where they find what Conte assumes to be Jed Kinter on the floor, feet tied together and hands tied behind his back, with a pillowcase, stained with what appears to be blood, tied around the head. The body lies motionless.

Conte is speechless, Rintrona says "Christ!" Tom says,

"Book 'em, Danno." Rintrona pokes the body with his foot. No response. Conte, with rising anger, says, "What have you goddamn done?"

Rintrona kicks the body with some force. No response. "Guy is really out."

"Tom?"

"Like I told you, Detective. I invited him to dinner. He comes down around 5:30. I offer him a glass of wine. I tell him, like you said, I might be coming down with something or it's my fuckin' allergies. That's how I said it, my fuckin' allergies, to relax him. He goes, I suffer from allergies too. I sympathize, Mr. Castellano. He's very polite with me, as usual. I say, I'm going to start the sausage and peppers. I had already browned the sausage before he came, to save time for the main event. I say, Make yourself at home, and give him a bottle of wine and the *O.D.* I say all this, like you said, in a bored voice. He starts reading about that woman who was murdered, he must've been, because he says, Too bad about that woman on Chestnut Street, I used to live in that neighborhood. I say, This town is getting worse and worse. He says nothing. We're pretty quiet after that. He uses the bathroom. When he gets back, after a long time I gotta say, he must have a gut problem, I serve the sausage and peppers. He compliments me excessively. Says his mother and wife can't cook a damn and that's why he has a second-rate stomach. I say, But I can, Jed. He looks at me in a way that's almost sad. Fuck you, I think. How about a second helping, son, I say. I work the father-son angle. He says, I'd love it. Now picture how I arranged him with his back to the stove. That's the crucial detail. I take his dish over. I put a second helping on his plate. I bring him the plate. I go back to the stove with my plate, he'll think I'm going for a second. The frying pan. You can test it out. It's giving me tendinitis over the years. It's a heavy fuckin' thing. Badda BOOM!!! With everything I got over the head. I tie him up good, as you observe. The bastard bleeds from the ears on my nice tile floor, which I paid through the nose for, so I get the pillow-case from the dirty laundry basket and that's about it. He's all yours, fellas, though I'm happy to lend a further hand."

Conte removes the pillowcase. Rintrona asks for ammonia and a rag. Castellano responds, "My pleasure." When Kinter starts to come to, Rintrona asks, "Now what, Eliot?" Conte tells him he'll pull into the driveway so they can put him into the trunk unobserved.

"Can I come with you and your friend, who I have yet to be introduced to?"

"From here on, Tom, you need to be insulated from the facts."

"Are you and your mysterious friend pleased with my work?"

"Anyone know you invited him for dinner?"

"Besides you and your unknown friend?"

"Right."

"No."

"Let's keep it that way."

Conte replaces the pillow-case as Kinter begins to babble meaninglessly. Before driving away, he calls Robinson, tells him about the photos, what Castellano found in the attic, the McPherson connection, that they have Kinter secured and are bringing him to the Savage Arms. They drive off. Thumping sounds from the trunk.

Rintrona says, "I thought for a minute he actually killed him, which would be okay except we'd have a problem with the body. What now, Eliot?"

Conte tells him they're going to a parking lot behind an abandoned factory on the edge of the city, where the chief of police will meet them. Rintrona says, "This is beginning to make me feel like a criminal. I'm thinking I should bow out."

"Want me to take you to your car?"

"Under no circumstances."

Conte parks behind the Savage Arms. Robinson is already there. The only light from a full moon. Robinson wants to know who the third party is. Conte tells him a "friend with experience, who shall remain nameless. Totally to be trusted."

"So where is he?"

Conte and Rintrona haul Kinter onto the broken pavement of weeds and broken glass, used condoms here and there, Kinter twisting and kicking his bound feet. Robinson says, "Keep the bag over his head. Let's have some privacy." They walk away, out of earshot. Robinson tells Conte that a video was forwarded to him that afternoon showing the plate of Conte's car and Conte himself entering the McPherson residence at the wrong time. A video taken by Kinter, "who must have tailed you there, and who obviously killed her."

"And who was too stupid," Eliot says, "to know that his address could not be hidden?"

"Not necessarily stupid, El."

"In the end," Rintrona adds, "it's their stupidity that's the nail in their coffin. Even the smartest of the worst of them are stupid in the end."

"Not necessarily. Your friend going to assist us tonight with speeches?"

"What are you implying, Robby?"

"I'm saying ever since that train incident your judgment is off. You're too emotional. What do we have? We have exactly nothing. The photos can't conclusively identify him as the substitute pallbearer. The platform shoes and revolver any shrewd lawyer will demonstrate can't be linked conclusively to Kinter. Maybe they were planted. Maybe Castellano was the substitute pallbearer, which is why they ended up in his attic. You get the picture? This is what I'm saying."

"But the DNA from the semen will definitively tie him to the murder. No lawyer can explain it away."

"Oh, yeah? The lawyer puts him on the stand and he testifies that he went over to say hello to his ex-landlady, who in fact invited him over, they got friendly, she fucked him, he leaves and you come into the picture. *Capeesh*? The video is used to nail *you*, which Kinter admittedly took because he feared for her when he's in the car and sees you pull up and enter – you, he testifies, who terrorized him violently on a train several days ago. You're a violent person. He sends me the video because he's a responsible citizen. Where does that leave us, El? Up shit creek without a paddle."

Rintrona speaks: "Mr. Robinson has it right. The son of a bitch walks."

Kinter thrashes on the broken pavement. Bleeds from both ears. Yelling.

"He kills Aristarco," Eliot says, "the Barbones, no doubt DePellaccio. And Nelson Thomas and – "

"He didn't kill Thomas. A witness got a partial on a plate. It was another drunken college kid. We brought him in and he confessed."

"Kinter kills Janice McPherson and walks? He does five murders, the first four I don't give a damn, nobody really does, but Janice McPherson I give a damn. He trailed me there. I brought him there, and he *walks*?"

"Just a second, gentleman," Robinson says, "I think I can fix the situation, but before I do, did you deal well with Michael C?"

"You're safe now."

Robinson goes over to Kinter, still thrashing, but quietly now. Robinson's back to Conte and Rintrona. Robinson crouches at Kinter's head. Can be heard speaking, softly, indistinctly. Kinter says, loudly, "Since when did you grow a pair?" Robinson fires four times through the pillowcase and through Kinter's brain. He stands, turns to Conte and Rintrona: "He doesn't walk. Satisfied, El? Satisfy your violent streak?"

Robinson removes two dropcloths from his trunk, wraps the body and drags it to the trunk. Says, "Hope your friend here is safe, El. Or else. I'll take care of the rest," drives off.

Rintrona says, "You can take me to my car now."

Conte says nothing.

"Your friend going to do me next?"

"He doesn't know your name. He doesn't know where you live. Only I know. Where did you park?"

"Only spot I could find was three blocks away."

"Good."

"Good?"

"He won't get your plate. Highly unlikely."

"In other words, he's thinking about doing me."

Conte says nothing.

"A Mafia thing all the way. Kinter thinks you're hot on the trail and Janet can link him up to the pallbearer. That's what it was."

Conte says nothing.

"The real question, Eliot? How does he know who you are? Where you live? Follows you around? To the McFarley residence? How does Kinter know these things? Christ, what have I involved myself in?"

Conte says nothing.

"Two final points and I'm outa here. He came with the dropcloths. The other point, if I'm you? Never turn your back on that man."

————————

At his front door, Conte finds a FedEx package. Return address: Laguna Beach, California. Tears it open, walks to the sidewalk, and under the street lamp reads:

Eliot,

Happy now that you FedExed the so-called transcript of Joan Dearborn's so-called phone call to destroy my marriage? This the same Joan Dearborn, by any chance, who you couldn't take your eyes off of when I was pregnant with our first child? But

you went too far, you son of a bitch, when you sent
a copy of your cruelty to the Laguna Beach Police,
who sent a well-built technician to acquire DNA
from Ralph's mouth, thank God he wasn't required
to shoot off into a cup for scientific reasons. Thanks
to you, I have detailed dirty pictures in my mind for
the rest of my days. Ralph is on his way. Have I mentioned Ralph bench-presses 325 pounds, you failed
flabby-assed academic? You'll never recognize him.
For all you know he's cruising Mary Street as you
read this. Our girls used to say (you remember them,
don't you?) Daddy Ralph, you are totally ripped, as
he walked around on a daily basis with his shirt off
in our home overlooking the ocean. After you run
into Ralph, I guarantee you'll wish you lived in a
world without mirrors.

Nancy

P.S. Still whining about your great father, I presume?

He hadn't sent a copy to the Laguna Beach Police and could
think of just two possibilities. The former Joan Dearborn or
Nancy herself. Conte is inclined to put his money on his ex.

CHAPTER 20

Late – no alcohol – little sleep. Three in the morning when the shock of Kinter's execution wears off and he's surprised by sympathy – even sadness for a man he had thought less than human.

9:00 A.M. The corridor toward his father's room. Coming at him, the executioner himself: "He wants you now, El. Just you. Are we surprised?"

"How is he, Robby?"

"Grateful for all I've done and for all that you didn't have to do, because I did."

"And you? Robby? How are you?"

"Everybody's safe now. We're all safe."

Pause. They stand uneasy in the silence.

"Coca won't trouble you again – guaranteed."

"It had to be his plan from way back when we were kids, El, don't you think?"

"What plan?"

"You wouldn't have to, because I would, to please the father who wasn't mine. And I did please him. Greatly. He had a plan, El, and I was it."

"You were always the favorite son, Robby."

"Fuck you."

"Fuck *me*? Really? You forget the time when Silvio ponied up The Golden Dago's fat fee? And Joe DiMaggio agrees to come to Utica? And Roofie goes for the lavish meal at Ventura's? Next day Joe and Silvio take to the links at Valley View. Silvio refuses a caddy but Joltin' Joe doesn't, at which point Silvio – that is to say, the man registered as my father – offers who else but you? The boy of the books, that's me, gets to shake the Yankee Clipper's hand at the first tee and watch you three go up the first fairway in a sea of midsummer green. You were his favorite, Robby. No question."

"I remember at Ventura's we ate grilled baby goat. *Capretto*, El."

"Yeah."

They embrace.

As Conte is about to enter his father's room, Robinson calls out, "Still on for this afternoon? *Bohème* with Pavarotti and Freni at their fuckin' peak? *Ossobuco alla Milanese*? What d'ya say, bro?" Conte shrugs, enters Silvio's room to find him in bed – IV, other monitors – apparently asleep.

Silvio opens his eyes. "They were supposed to bring me a Coke an hour ago. They didn't come across."

"I'll get you one."

"No."

"It's just down the hall."

"Talk to me."

"I'll get the Coke first."

"Stay. Please. (Pause.) There was no plan."

"You heard him say that?"

Silvio smiles.

"I'll die today."

"No you won't."

 Pause.

"You always loved to contradict me. What else is new?"

"Sorry."

"Your best quality. It saved you. (Pause.) We'll see, if you're saved. I won't be, of course."

"I could do better."

 He coughs. "Hold my hand."

 Eliot does.

"Don't let go, Eliot."

"I won't."

 Pause.

"What a catastrophe."

"What?"

"Time."

 Pause.

"I'm here, Dad."

"Never had any for you."

 Eliot does not respond.

"You were always interested in storybooks. Reading at the table. The book in your lap. (Pause.) You're a reader. Beautiful."

"But you've got the stories. Unruh, Bobby, JFK – tell me another one."

 Silvio looks away. Extended silence.

"The Barbones were the story. Salvatore and Bad Frank."

"Tell me."

"Sin City of the East cleaned up, their proceeds run down. They come to me."

"Why?"

"Squeeze city contracts. For them. Scum."

"Tell it all."

"They gave me an ultimatum."

"Or?"

"Or else."

"Or else they?"

"Raise up the back of my bed. Thank you."

"What did you do?"

"Did I give in, you mean?"

"Did you?"

"That's what they thought."

Eliot says nothing.

"Save my own ass and my minorities lose their jobs? Yeah, sure, Sal, give me a couple of months. Just two months and I'll make you and Frank very happy. So. (Pause. Finding his breath.) So. (Pause.) Talked to an intermediary, is that the word? You know all the words, Eliot. (Pause.) So. Intermediary tells me no can do. Small fish, the Barbones. Minnows."

"Don't tell me you contacted someone connected?"

"Yes. I'm telling you. A month later the intermediary gets in touch. Aristarco, Aristarco is coming to Utica. (Pause.) Albert the Whale. In addition, we'll do the Barbones for you. Seventy-five grand."

"What are you telling me?"

"My best story. Rhode Island sends Kinter. Providence sends him. There's a word for us, Eliot. 'Providence.' Patriarca's city has the right name, don't you think?"

"You sponsored him? You're telling me that?"

"Yes."

"Who bribed DePellaccio?"

"I did."

"DePellaccio knew what he was getting into?"

"No. He knew only to have back spasms. Poor bastard."

"Kinter killed him?"

"Good guess."

"Who told him to?"

"His own initiative, leave it at that."

"Leave it at that?"

"Jed wanted a new life."

"Jed? A first-name basis?"

"Got him a job through Whitaker. Gave him his rent and then some. Every month. Cash."

"Or he would?"

"Of course."

"*Kill* you?"

"Worse."

"What?"

"Expose."

"Who told Robby to crash the bus?"

"Your dear father. Providence sent Jed, but I was the engineer. I designed it all."

"Robby's been in contact with Kinter all along?"

Pause.

"It would seem so. Leave it at that."

"Janice McPherson?"

"Kinter. Or a sex maniac. I believe a sex maniac."

"How does Kinter know about me?"

"You know."

"Robby?"

"Yes."

"Kinter kills Janice to save you and Robby from exposure?"

"If he did it."

"On Big Daddy's orders?"

"No, never. She was not within my design."

"Who told him to? Robby?"

"I will never believe that. Forget that thought forever. Robby is a good man."

"Was Kinter going to do me eventually?"

"No."

"Why not?"

Pause.

"Trust me, if you can. He feared Robby."

"Robby killed him last night. Do you know this?"

"Of course."

"Your doctor, who vouched for DePellaccio's phony back spasm? Ronald Sheehan. Kinter?"

Pause.

"That was a tragedy. A great man."

"Kinter again. Right?"

"I never authorized that."

"But he did it anyway. Right?"

"An accident, we hope."

The Coke arrives.

"Help me, Eliot. Hold it. Thank you."

Silvio recovers energy that had seemed forever lost, a fierceness now visible, to tell his last story:

"That poor devil, Michael Coca, a failure in business many times, but a decent person with an unfortunate name – your mother, did you know, was distantly related to him? There's some Caca in your blood, Eliot. The last venture before I sent him with Antonio in their mid-thirties to the police academy was the Clinic for Italian-American Mental Health. Don't laugh. Coca says, Mr. Conte, we Italians are wonderful people, but our heads are not screwed on tight. I had to agree. My head was always a little tilted. We need, he says, special therapy in the context of our explosive heritage. Will you help? I made a nice contribution. Tragically, the only psychiatrists he found were two old Jews, and that was that. Don't laugh."

He closes his eyes. Pauses for thirty seconds.

"After the sad injury that destroyed his chance for a pro career, Antonio was doomed to coach at Proctor High for some years... unhappy watching those kids play lousy the game he could no longer play. My plan was to have them rise together. Which they did. To be at my disposal down the road. But after the Aristarco business, I made the choice of Antonio. Antonio was always in the cards for my personal chief of police. Let's face it, it had to be that way – Antonio over Michael, the second banana, who was in the cards to be my backup should anything ever happen, including backup in the van if Antonio, our gentle Antonio, lost his nerve, Michael would take over the van, Michael was in on the plan from the start. Jealousy sets in, it tends to, of course, and after a point the second banana couldn't take lagging behind. That point was reached a couple of weeks ago. I'm tired, Eliot... It was not in my design to hurt Michael. Until you called him to the Savage Arms last night with Jed in the trunk of your car, Antonio never hurt a flea. He killed him. Yes. Let's be totally honest on my deathbed. You know enough law to know you didn't have the legal goods and in the back of your mind that's why you called Antonio to that forsaken place. He came prepared with the dropcloths to do what you in your heart wanted done, but couldn't do. Don't bullshit yourself on that point. You brought Kinter to the Savage to die."

Long pause.

"I set it in motion fifteen years ago. I did it. I was the designer. Me. Now it's over in the best way and we three pay with the knowledge of what we three wanted."

"You were the spider at the center of the web."

"You were always good with words, Eliot."

"Why have you told me all this? Why now?"

"You're smart. You tell me."

"I want to hear it from you."

"To set you free. What else?"

"From?"

"Me."

"You must be joking. You actually believe that?"

"Are you, Eliot? Free?"

"Is that a serious question?"

"Have patience. You'll see. Something else. If I thought you were interested in Tootsie, I'd be worried."

"Why?"

"She's your half-sister. After your mother, I fell in love with Angie Tomasi."

"Christ, what else do you have in store for me? Tootsie knows this? Jesus Christ."

"Yes. Tootsie knows for a long time."

"Why?"

Pause.

"Thought it would keep her from having the wrong feelings for you. How stupid of me."

"Did you ever cheat on Mom?"

"Never."

"Ever want to?"

"We want bad things at times. Doesn't mean we do them. I wanted one very bad thing, and I did it."

"You authorize or you don't authorize. You design. My God, Dad."

"You've got a terrible temper, Eliot. (Pause. Weakly:) Don't cross the line with it."

"Anything else?"

"Hold my hand."

Pause. Softly:

"I've been holding it."

"Love Robby. Love your brother come hell or high water."

"I think we're drowning in hell, Big Daddy. You, me, Robby."

Silvio smiles a big smile, "That's my boy!"

"But I never – "

"Don't" (wracking wet cough) "bullshit yourself."

Tootsie enters: "My favorite two guys in the world, together again at last. Hey! I'm head over heels!"

———————

In the parking lot of Saint Elizabeth's, in the car, Conte checks his BlackBerry. Message: CCruz.

E – my daughter in auto accident early this morning.

Banged up in hospital. She's okay. Need to be with her today. Relieved she's not in danger and seriously disappointed not to be coming to you. Rain check. Please. Soon. – C.

He responds:

Not as disappointed as I am. Rain check good any-time any day always. Come soon as you can. – E.

His excited anticipation of her arrival now crashed – how does he divert himself from his father's revelations? Drives home and goes directly to bed at 10:30 A.M. Awakes at noon, more fatigued than before, and calls Antonio Robinson. Leaves message:

Come over for *Bohème* and long lunch. Please.

Imagines a call to Laguna Beach: "Let's finally have shared custody, Nancy. Send me half the ashes."

At 1:00, Antonio enters without knocking, with a box of cookies, a loaf of bread, and two six packs of Excaliber. Eliot in the kitchen chopping the parsley and working on the garlic with a razor. Transparent slivers. Robinson says, "I'm here, brother." Conte nods, "I'm glad you're here. More than you know."

"Silvio tell you a story? Why beat around the bush?"

"He did, he really did."

"He said he would."

"Told me everything. Can't say I'm clear on every point."

"You want to be? Because I could – "

"No."

"Sure?"

"Yes."

"Want to talk about any of it?"

"No."

"Any word from Laguna Beach?"

"Nothing. Would you mind opening a bottle of that crap I drink now?"

"My favorite thing now too. We're joining forces, El."

They toast each other.

Eliot says, "You're a good man, Charlie Brown. Don't ever tell yourself otherwise."

"That an example of your sick humor? How can we believe that?"

"I'm glad you're here, Robby."

"Cain and Abel. We're not those guys."

"Never heard of them, Robby. Utica boys?"

"They were lousy brothers."

"Because they weren't Utica boys, Mr. Robinson."

"Unlike us, Mr. Conte. But what about Tom and Ricky Castellano? They're Utica boys *and* lousy brothers."

Eliot at the stove: "The meal won't feature what I promised you. When? Last Saturday?"

"No *Ossobuco* and so forth?"

"Spaghetti in that tuna sauce you like so much. You want to put the antipasto together? The salami and provolone are waiting for you in the refrigerator. Artichoke hearts in there too in olive oil, and those olives you go for."

"I brought the bread from Napoli's."

"Hungry?"

"I could eat a – I don't know what."

"Me too."

"A week ago today we were in Troy for the *Carmen* I didn't stay for. If I had only stayed…"

"Not a week ago, El. And forget 'if,' as Silvio always says."

"Sure it was."

"Technically, eight days. Saturday to Saturday. Right? Eight days."

"Yeah, you're right. But a week sounds better, don't you think? You want to start listening now or after?"

"How about we play the two duets with the antipasto?"

"'O soave fanciulla' and 'Addio senza rancor?'" (Oh, sweet girl and Goodbye, without hard feelings.)

"Yeah, El, but let's reverse the order."

"How come?"

"Finish with romantic expectation and the happiness that lies just ahead."

"When they sing that I get goose bumps, though I've heard it a hundred times."

"That fucker Puccini, El. I get the chills. Makes the hair on my arms stand up. Every time."

"How about you do the antipasto while I make the sauce. Okay?"

"I brought the cookies from Ricky. Unlike you last Saturday, I didn't forget."

"I knew I could count on you, Robby."

"You can."

"Every time."

"Every time."

They eat and drink slowly, in silence. The antipasto is good. The aroma of the simmering sauce is good. The only sounds the clinking of utensils.

"We'll plan it together, Robby."

"What's that?"

"Our father's wake and funeral."

"Thanks, El."

"For what?"

"For saying it that way."

Eliot looks at him quizzically.

"You said our father. You never said it before."

"Let's try to figure this out, Robby. He's my father and you're my brother, are you not? Therefore, he's?"

"Our father."

Antonio Robinson clears the antipasto plates and sets the table for the main course, while Eliot Conte drains the steaming pasta – as the surge of the preferred duet fills the house. Conte at the stove is now spooning the tuna sauce into the steaming pot of drained pasta. Robinson from behind him is reaching into his pocket. Conte is now mixing the sauce thoroughly through the strands of drained pasta. Robinson, hand still in pocket, is hesitating. He's glancing at the back of Conte's head. Conte is still at the stove, back to his brother, when Robinson quickly withdraws it and places it silently alongside Conte's plate. The missing BlackBerry.

THANKS TO

Christopher Celenza, Director, and his splendid staff at the American Academy in Rome, where I finished the manuscript during two magically productive weeks.

Ⓜ MELVILLE INTERNATIONAL CRIME